T0160885

RED HOLLER

Editors

John Branscum

Wayne Thomas

CONTEMPORARY

APPALACHIAN

LITERATURE

THE LINDA BRUCKHEIMER PRIZE IN KENTUCKY LITERATURE

Sarabande Books

LOUISVILLE, KENTUCKY

Library of Congress Cataloging-in-Publication Data

Red holler : contemporary Appalachian literature / edited by John E. Branscum and
Wayne Thomas.—First edition.
   pages cm
 Summary: A diverse anthology of poetry, fiction, nonfiction, and graphic essays by
contemporary Appalachian writers. The editors have assembled a collection spanning
ten years and the mountain range from Mississippi to New York, placing fresh new
voices alongside widely known and celebrated authors. From Native American myth,
African American urban legend, folk culture, and European ghost stories, this is an
anthology of disenfranchised, yet robust peoples — Provided by publisher.
  ISBN 978-1-936747-66-5 (pbk. : alk. paper)
  1. American literature—Appalachian Region. 2. Appalachian Region—Literary collections. 3. American literature—21st century. 4. Appalachian Region—Civilization.
I. Branscum, John E., 1970– editor of compilation. II. Thomas, Wayne, 1976– editor of
compilation. III. Title: Contemporary Appalachian literature.
PS537.R43 2013
810.8'0974—dc23
               2013005924

Cover and text design by Kirkby Gann Tittle.

Manufactured in Canada.

This book is printed on acid-free paper.

Sarabande Books is a nonprofit literary organization.

This project is supported in part by an award from the National
Endowment for the Arts.

The Kentucky Arts Council, the state arts agency, supports
Sarabande Books with state tax dollars and federal funding from
the National Endowment for the Arts.

CONTENTS

FOREWORD

WE GREW UP WITH STORIES. Stories of Dixie Mafia uncles with black
fedoras pulled low over cold nickel eyes. Stories of teenage housing project witches. Stories of poverty by the railroad tracks where rats go after
babies' toes at night. Stories of ill-fated, whiskey-fueled love that crosses
color, gender, and county lines. These stories give our world shape and
edge and tell us who we are and whence we came. The work we've
selected for *Red Holler* recasts and builds on these tales from our youth,
and, in doing so, comprises a revolutionary twenty-first century portrait
of the region.

Forget the clichés about toothless farmers and banjo music, unedu-
cated coal miners, and incestuous barefoot children. *Red Holler* show-
cases an Appalachia that is a racially-mixed explosive contact zone
between urban and rural sensibilities, a culture as in love with hip-hop
and heavy metal as it is country and bluegrass, and a people as likely to
roost and hustle in Pittsburgh housing projects as they are in Eastern
Kentucky trailer parks.

Here, you'll find Jeff Mann's "715 Wiley Street," a poignant and
funny coming-of-age memoir in which the author reflects back on his
years as a gay college undergraduate. Brian Barker's "In the City of
Fallen Rebels" recounts the surrealistic journey of a boy dragging death
by a string in a world of "light raked loose." Jacinda Townsend's

"Lackland" chronicles a young black soldier's battle with his bedeviled feet and bedeviled heart on a Texas army base. Alex Taylor's "Lakeside Penitence" offers an uncanny gothic tale of sexual perversion, mourning, and noodling gone wrong. Donald Ray Pollock's "Real Life" gives us a son who learns the gospel of blood and teeth at the local drive-in.

Here, you'll gain renewed appreciation for ornery, anti-authoritarian, and irreverent Appalachian sensibilities, which lampoon and interrogate mainstream attitudes about everything from sex to race. You'll be treated to outlaw black humor, as rooted in a blunt celebration of the body as it is in a fatalistic awareness of how fast favorable circumstances can turn. You'll encounter works by such writers as Maurice Manning, Pinckney Benedict, Ally Reeves, Jane Springer, and Bianca Spriggs that celebrate our kinship with the natural order's fierce violences and pleasures and excitedly mine the magical realist and surrealist veins of Appalachian literature.

Appalachian literature is some of the most important literature in America. It is a literature of the dispossessed that has laid bare the social, psychological, and spiritual struggles of the people who have fought to survive in America's economic and social borderlands since its inception. These are not regional tales of a disappearing age. These are harrowing and hilarious stories that redefine our ever-changing landscape and expectations for the new century. *Red Holler* is a celebration, a hell-raising, a storming of field and street; it is more enchanted mountain wood stoking the fire in eyes that just won't quit seeing, mouths that just won't quit hungering, and spirits that refuse to back down. Enjoy.

John Branscum, Indiana, PA
Wayne Thomas, Tusculum, TN

INTRODUCTION

HERE'S A SCENE FROM A BARBERSHOP in my hometown in Greenbrier County, West Virginia, a memory from my young manhood, a time now long gone. You can easily imagine the place—the scissors and combs and cutthroat razor submerged in glass vats of blue Barbicide (*Disinfectant, Fungicide & Virucide*) on the counter along the back wall; the dark ancient wood, the great dusty mirrors, the photographs of long-deceased Greenbrier Countians hanging from the walls; the pile of well-thumbed glossy magazines, their covers decorated with scantily-clad girls in contorted postures, because this is a place of men.

I'm sitting in one of the hard wooden seats that line the walls of the place, waiting for my turn in the barber's chair. There are two such chairs but only one barber, a sweet guy and former Navy man, who has cut my hair since I was a boy; hence the wait is often quite long, and the longer the better, so far as I am concerned. It's a pleasant spring day, and the barbershop is, as it almost invariably is, populated by elderly loafers, some of them there for a haircut, most just hanging around for the company and the conversation.

These guys have known each other for decades, for generations, most of them veterans of one war or another, so that a lot of their conversation centers on trips to the VA hospital in Roanoke, Virginia, not far away. One of the oldest of them was a frogman, an underwater demolitions expert, during the Second World War. They are some pretty hard old pine knots.

Past the front windows of the place, down the sidewalk of the main street of the town, floats a vision in a filmy dress. The barbershop loafers are accustomed to observing women as they go by the front of the place and commenting on their merits, imagined and observed, and they watch this apparition stroll past as usual; but the dress is not worn by a woman. I have said the word "dress," but the only description, really, is *frock*, a spring frock in some delicate pattern. It's pretty.

The dude wearing the frock is, putting it kindly, not pretty. He's broad across the shoulders, burly and hairy-chested, sporting an impressive lumberjack's beard. I am in college by this point in my life and thus less shocked by the sight of a man wearing a dress than I might once have been, but these fellows are, I feel confident, less liberal about such things than I am. I have been *elsewhere*. I am pleased to think that I am sophisticated.

So the Paul Bunyan type in the pretty gown promenades by, and the loafers watch as they might watch anybody passing the windows of their little club, and then they go back to their previous conversation. And Gene notices me gawping.

"That was Earl _____," he says to me in a reassuring tone, and I recognize the last name as belonging to the area. "He decided a while ago that he just felt more comfortable wearing women's clothes." And the other fellows pipe up. It turns out that Earl is related to at least two guys in the room, comes from a family that's lived in the region since around the time of the Revolution. He's a hard worker, they tell me. From various parts of the room comes a list of Earl's bona fides. His virtuous service in one branch or another of the military. His abiding faith in Christ, which does not necessarily alter just because a man changes his sartorial preferences. And I realize they're worried that I will think ill of Earl, who is for better or worse one of them, who is part of this place. They vouch for him. They love him.

Appalachia: land of marvelous contradiction. Land of the contrarian, who never fails to surprise you by the energy and inventiveness with which he resists you and your notion of him. Where, as Freud put it when writing about the human id, "contrary impulses exist side by side, without cancelling each other out."

In Appalachia, no possibility cancels out any other.

They have seen and undergone a great deal, these old gray fellows now ranged around the periphery of the barbershop. A number of them grew up without electricity or running water. They might not have much to show for it, but they've worked, and worked hard, all their lives. They've fought in the South Pacific and at the Chosin Reservoir and at Khe Sanh. These ancient ridges among which they've lived their lives, when not off fighting the nation's wars, couldn't care less what a man wears as he glides down Washington Street. They have been here since the dawn of time. The men in Flanagan's barbershop have been here only a little less long, as it seems to me, and they couldn't care less either.

I don't believe I ever went into that barbershop that I didn't come out with a story of some sort that I wanted to tell. Stories about men who killed themselves with sticks of dynamite, and stories about men sentenced to the state maximum-security prison at Moundsville without the possibility of parole. Stories about women who stabbed the men who loved them; about brothers, one of whom went around the world and the other who never left the shadow of the knob where he was born, and both of them died within an hour of each other.

A whole lifetime of such stories, so that I hardly mind now that I am bald and no longer in need of a barbershop, nor that I live over six hundred miles away from that once-familiar place, nor that it is now under new ownership and all of the old loafers who used to linger there and swap tales are now dead, like the men in the photos on the walls.

I hardly mind that the town, which was a sleepy pleasant cow-town when I was growing up, the long-time residents all agricultural people well known to me and my family, is now overrun with lawyers and doctors, the new princes of the realm, and by tourists who drift in gaggles from quilt store to charming quilt store, marveling at the town's quaintness and the undeniable beauty of its setting, there along the big levels of the Greenbrier Valley.

I hardly mind at all.

I have found, as a born-and-bred Appalachian who has spent much of his adult life outside the region, and who has found himself on more than one occasion a reluctant (even unwilling) ambassador for and representative of the Appalachian region and culture, that folks from elsewhere will believe almost anything you tell them about the place. The gaudier and weirder the tale is, the better they like it and the more true it seems to them. Sometimes the impulse to pull their legs is irresistible, and I find myself embarked on some epic fantasia of violence and twisted sexuality. In such circumstances, I am in heaven. I am a writer. I am a liar. So sue me.

Appalachia is America's literary id. It is the place where every monstrous or dreamlike thing seems possible, where every carnal fantasy may realize itself unimpeded by human laws, by technology ("Why, these hills seems to be blocking my cell-phone signal. However shall I call for help?"), or by the ever-advancing tide of the generic and the universally familiar. Do we, the natives of the region, and those of us who tell its stories—do we sometimes suffer for it? Yes. But ours is a necessary and even a desirable sacrifice. Appalachia stands like a bulwark: contemporary America's escape from the terrible panopticon of bland modernity.

Thus this anthology (likewise necessary) of Appalachian prose, poetry, and graphic narratives in which every element of Appalachian mythology is examined and turned on its head, made new and surprising by the skill and imagination of the artists involved, who are among the best that Appalachia has—has ever had—to offer. I knew those old men in that barbershop, had known them all my life, as you, reader, perhaps know Appalachia. And still they managed to surprise me by their capacity for wisdom, love, and real acceptance for and tolerance of— more than tolerance: positive enthusiasm for—human nature, with all its quirks and oddities and foibles, as well as its unexpected softness and prettiness and grace.

Just so will the work collected in this marvelous book surprise and delight you, while contradicting everything you imagine you know. Perhaps you will even feel a bit humbled by it, as I felt then in the presence of those tough, loving old men, and as I feel now in the presence of these phenomenal talents.

Welcome to Appalachia. Welcome to *Red Holler*.

—Pinckney Benedict

Red Holler

Nin Andrews

What the Dead See

after Frank Stanford

Back then I never let on. Besides, no one was there to set the record
straight, the womb I fell from, soused with liquor. And there was any
kind of excuse. I was younger then than I ever knew, in air swimming
with insects. Sometimes, talking with the Baptist preacher on the patio
about the folks who have gone from this world, I felt them, like they
were fish bones caught in my throat. *The dead have things*, he'd say*, they
don't even let on to the devil they know. The living does too.* Like my head
was a transistor radio, he wanted to find that gospel station, make me
fear the Lord. His breath, warm on my face, a whiff of fish thawing,
the rain like small feet on the lake. I'd watch it and sip from a green
Co-Cola bottle slowly, wondering what the Lord and the devil don't
know, seeing nobody seeing us. Nights, when my folks came home
late, the headlights crossed my ceiling. Shadows kept falling and falling. I'd watch my sister's boyfriend slip out. She was good at faking
shit, like sleep, like caring what she did. Afterwards, I'd listen. Sometimes the dark would look at itself and sigh, and the wind would blow
in the alfalfa field. I'd hear someone whispering so soft, no one heard
her words.

Sundays

sitting beneath the fan in the kitchen,
the blade shadows going over
and over my face,

I listened to the gospel on the radio,
some Baptist preacher saying
it was high time
we learned to walk right
with the Lord. The sin
can seep from the body
like oil from a rusty can.

Wasps crawled over and over
the bruised plums in the bowl
on the kitchen table.
When the hymns began,
I picked burdock from my kneesocks
and hummed along.
Bobby Jones, the hired kid from town,
came up from the horse barn,
plucked a floating egg
from a jar of pickle juice
on the counter, the dirt
from his fingers rising
in a dark cloud.

We never said a word.
Afterwards, I watched him
head down the gravel road to the stalls,
his body-glide inside his clothes
like some kind of music
riding his skin.
I didn't want to let on
I was looking.
That's how much I liked him.

A Brief History of Melvin, My Own Personal Bull

1.

Little girls shouldn't own bulls, my mother said, looking doubtfully at Melvin, a small, sickly calf on the day he is born. But my dad said I was special. *Yes,* he said to me, *Melvin can be your own personal bull.*

2.

I slept in the barn that summer, nursing Melvin back to health. My father said I was learning responsibility. My mother said I needed to wash the dirt from behind my ears and beneath my fingernails.

3.

That was the year of the drought. Not a drop of rain fell in July and August, and heat lightning lit up the sky night after night. The alfalfa turned from yellow to brown, and the red dirt became as hard as a rock. My parents fought about the price of food and farm equipment, the Vietnam War, and what they would do if my brother was drafted. And my love affair with a baby bull. *Are you going to be the one to explain it to her?* my mother would ask in a threatening voice.

4.

Nights I dreamt of running away. I'd wait until Melvin grew up. Then I'd take a canteen of water, my mom's MasterCard, and Melvin. I knew I'd be safe with Melvin, my own personal bull, by my side.

5.

Melvin grew strong, and by fall he weighed about 1000 pounds. I played tag with him after school, waving burlap bags in the air as if they were red flags. Melvin charged and charged, always stopping short in a cloud of dirt, and rubbing his nose on my blouse.

6.

I wrote stories for my third-grade teacher in which Melvin was the star. He speared murderers and thieves with his horns. He outran wolves and cop cars. When I grew tired, he let me ride on his back. The teacher said girls don't ride bulls. Bulls won't allow it. But she had never met Melvin, my own personal bull.

7.

The farmhand complained that Melvin was dangerous. The vet agreed. He said little girls shouldn't play with bulls. My father worried. My mother said, *I told you so.*

8.

I came home from a school camping trip, and Melvin was gone. My dad said Melvin had been sent to another farm where there were other bulls and cows his own size to play with. My mother said, *Your father tells lies.*

9.

We ate steak night after night. My mother chewed happily, wiping the grease on her napkin. *They say that love makes the meat rich and sweet,* she said. *It's true. Isn't it, Love?*

10.

My father pushed his plate away and turned white. *Don't talk to your food*, he said, banging his fist on the table. My mother laughed and laughed.

11.

Hello, Melvin, I said again, stabbing a forkful of pink meat and holding it up to the light. *Now, don't you look lovely tonight?* Then I took another bite.

Makalani Bandele

southbound #71

boarding the bus, change drops out of your pocket and goes every which way like feet tangled up in loose shoestrings or the feathers of the sparrow that has smashed into a plate glass window twenty stories up. the fare machine doesn't ding, and that's all the money you have. the bus driver looks at you like you just picked your nose and wiped it on your shirt, and directs you rearward; you're now another reason she hates this route. an older black woman looks asleep, except for her arms floating gently in the air as if directing a choir. a red, blue, and white man in a hoveround reminds you it's the fourth of july. curly hair-prints in a grease stain on the window. pink chewing gum in the only empty seat. incessant beeping, the bus transmission is overheating. crumpled-up brown bag rolls up and down the aisle. the woman you are going to sleep with tonight reads the impending fare hikes. she has not noticed you yet.

 coming off the second street bridge, the bus turns onto main street and the city busts open like a ripe watermelon fallen off a truck: asphalt, people, glass, steel, cars, and concrete everywhere. this young brother is a throwback to the 1940s taking up his usual spot in the back of the bus, until you realize he has the best seat if you are curious and like to watch. everyone on here knows where they're not going, the bus number predetermined that.

even when you drive yourself to work, you don't know her before you depart, though you always end up on your back looking up at the effort in her face to derive some pleasure out of all of this.

Brian Barker

Visions for the Last Night on Earth

Then I saw the floodwaters recede, leaving a milky scum
scalloped on silos and billboards, and the eaves of farmhouses
were festooned with a mossy brown riverweed
that hung in the August heat like bankers' limp fingers,
and the drowned corn, sick from sewage and tidesuck,
reappeared like a washed-out green ocean of wilting speartips
that bloated fish rode into the moonlight,
and the lost dogs came down from the hills, still lost,
trotting, panting, a tremolo of swollen tongues, their mudcaked
undercarriages swarmed by squadrons of gnats
as dilapidated barns began disappearing at last, swallowed like secrets
by the muck, and the ghosts of handsome assassins
sat up in piles of hay and combed their pompadours
and muttered in Latin their last prayers
before stepping through trapdoors flung open
like flaps of skullskin to the skyblue sky of oblivion—

that same color of your panties, I thought, as you floated topless
across our bedroom in a wake of sparks, a vision sashaying
across the bottom of the sea, visions colliding, the sea rising, please
    forgive me
my terrors, love, for I saw your braided hair and imagined
a frayed rope lowered from a helicopter, or, worse,
the ropey penis of the horse a general sits on in the shade
as bluebottle flies, querulous and fierce, baffle the air
above silhouettes bent digging in a field of clay.
For I watched the sunset so many evenings, holding your hand,

and thought of the combustible blood of an empire,
or lay awake in the long dark listening to your breathing
and imagined sad Abe Lincoln pacing our hallway, his arms folded
behind his back like a broken umbrella, the clock ticking,
the ravenblack sedans idling curbside in the suburbs
of America, watching closely, purring greedily,
as they gulped down the last starlight, dreaming of some other dawn.

In the City of Fallen Rebels

—after Jaime Sabines

Here comes the boy again, dragging his death
by a string. Here comes the gun he waves above his head.
Here comes the light raked loose
like salted slugs, how it fizzes over liquor bottles
and magazine racks, and he must feel it, yes,
like ulcers puckering his skin, for he hugs himself
with his other arm, high-stepping in place, trying to hold in
the filthy, burst mattress of the soul.
But here it comes nonetheless! Christ, look at it!
It won't stop jumping out
to bang on the scuffed Plexiglas window
of heaven. Here come the angels,
they hear him, those starved revenants
trampling the riverbank of his mind. But the gods,
they refuse to blink, *He's nothing more*
than a speck of shit on the eyelash of infinity, they say,
spitting sideways into the dust,
though they come anyway, like Confederate marauders
spurring their wormy, wide-eyed horses
up from the shallow graves.
They're peat-burnt and staunch, they're flashing their bleary sabers.

One has a face that keeps fuzzing out,
and one has biceps like a pit bull's flanks splattered with blood,
and when he shoots at them, wailing, bottles explode,
rum tumbles down shelves, trickles
toward the feet of Mrs. Wen.
Here she comes too, fumbling the keys,
trying to coax the register open.
Here come the five English words she knows,
flitting about her like flying mice.
Here come the gods again (They never give up),
and the boiling sargassum of blood she can't hold inside her chest,
as some fusty, ferruginous fog blows in
from the backside of the ghetto.
Here come the dead, they smell it, waking in vacant lots,
shoeless and soft in the weeds. Here come
the screwworms and roaches, the black ocean seething in its bowl
and a whole century like a ship on fire.
In the park, where the boy buys his tinfoil surprise,
the severed heads of history nod all night on their rotten branches.
He blows the gates. He sleeps
his dreamless sleep, curled fetal beneath a bench,
his eyelids blue and blotched with bruises.
Here comes the poet (What does *he* want?).
He's scared of the dark; he'd like to turn into a sparrow,
fly into a steeple, hide beneath a broken bell.
But a desiccated bat hangs at the back of his mind.
He keeps poking it with his pen until the godawful
gods come again (They never quit!).
Here they come, galloping across the river
of a dead king rising, surpliced, bearded in flames,
blowing their battered bugles.
They want a word with the boy, they say. They take him
into the trees. And there he goes, still half-asleep,
dragging his death by a string.

ORgo vs the Flatlanders

BY PINCKNEY BENEDICT

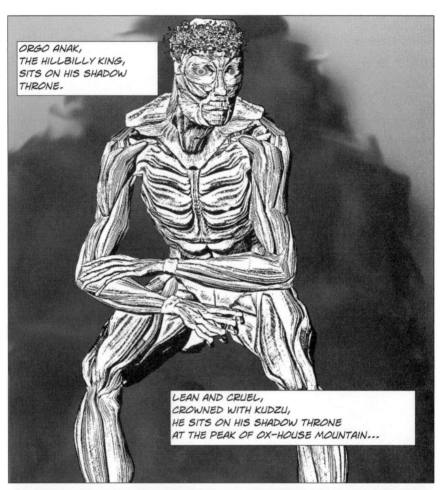

ORGO ANAK,
THE HILLBILLY KING,
SITS ON HIS SHADOW
THRONE.

LEAN AND CRUEL,
CROWNED WITH KUDZU,
HE SITS ON HIS SHADOW THRONE
AT THE PEAK OF OX-HOUSE MOUNTAIN...

...AND HE WAITS.

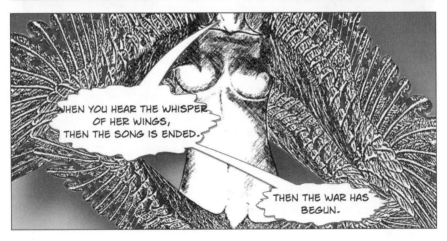

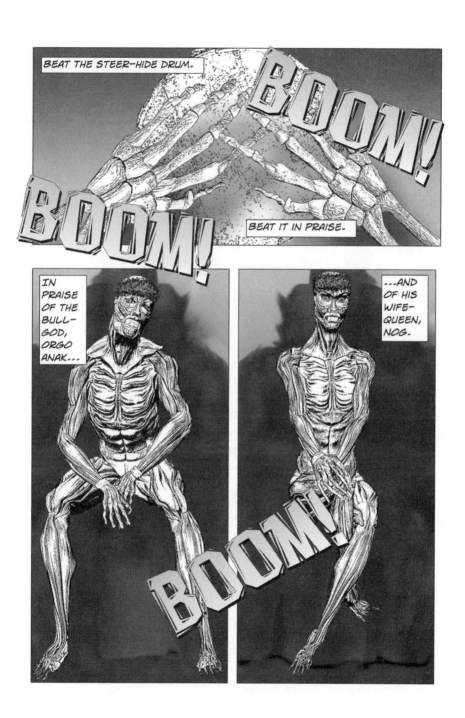

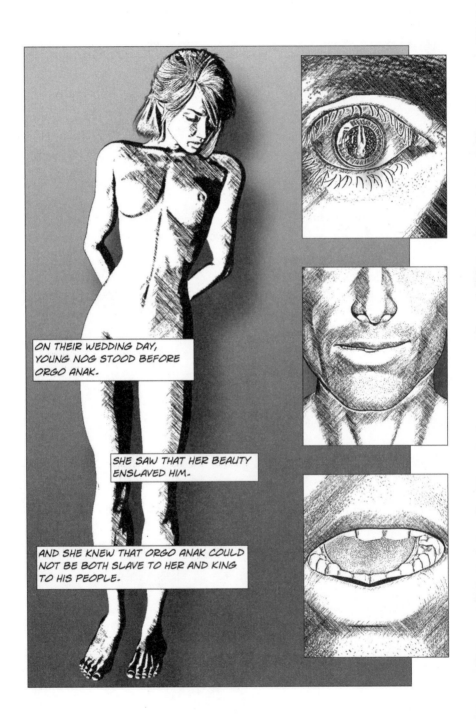

ON THEIR WEDDING DAY,
YOUNG NOG STOOD BEFORE
ORGO ANAK.

SHE SAW THAT HER BEAUTY
ENSLAVED HIM.

AND SHE KNEW THAT ORGO ANAK COULD
NOT BE BOTH SLAVE TO HER AND KING
TO HIS PEOPLE.

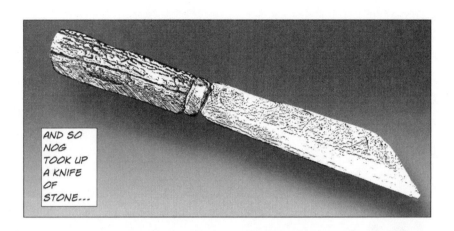

AND SO NOG TOOK UP A KNIFE OF STONE...

...AND PEELED HER OWN SKIN AWAY.

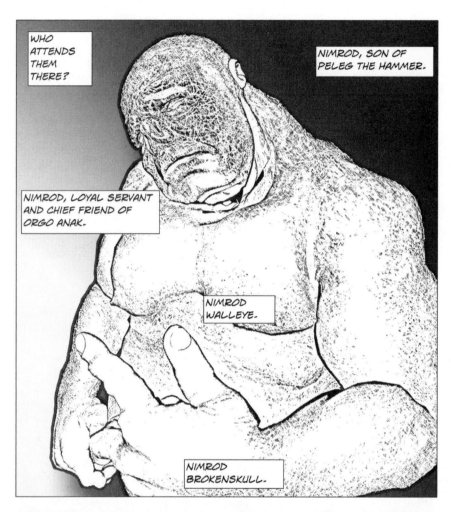

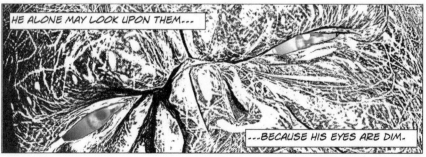

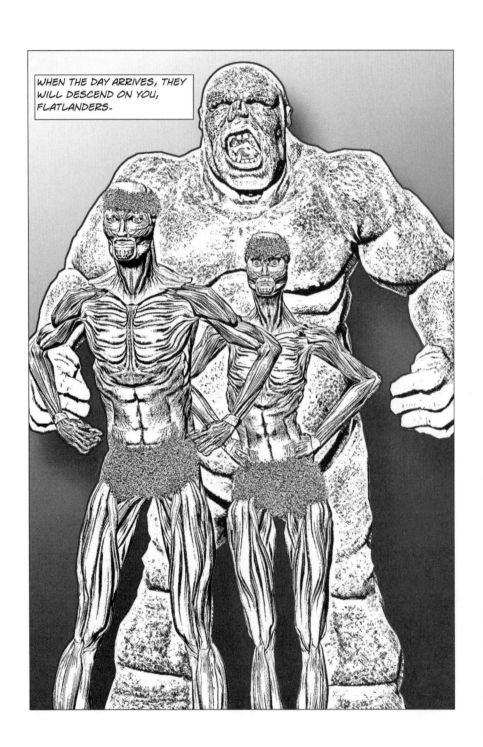

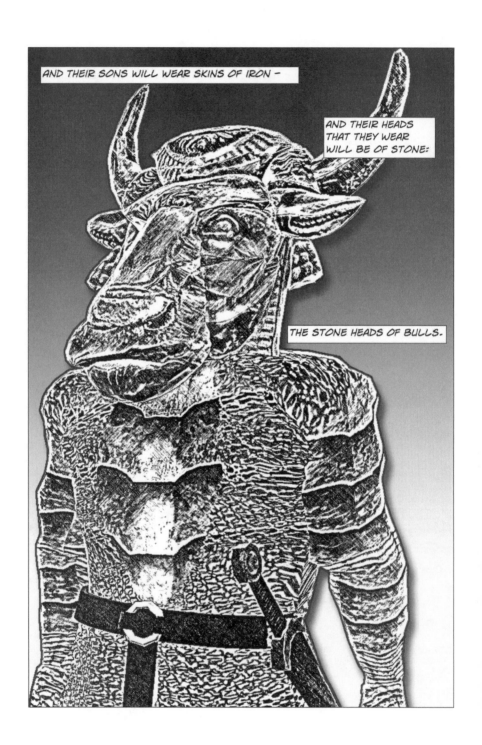

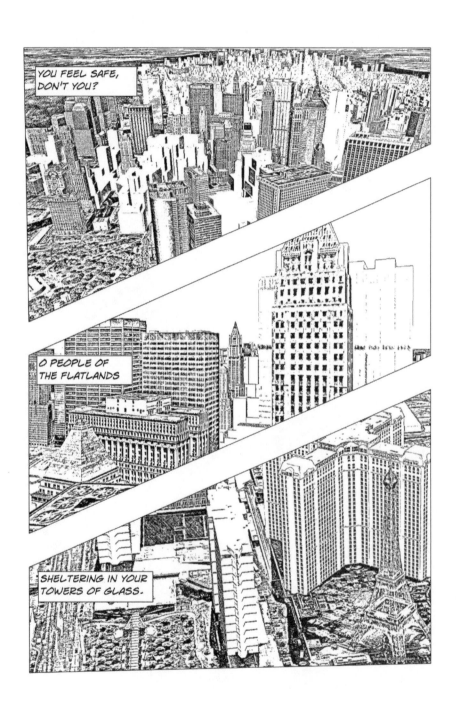

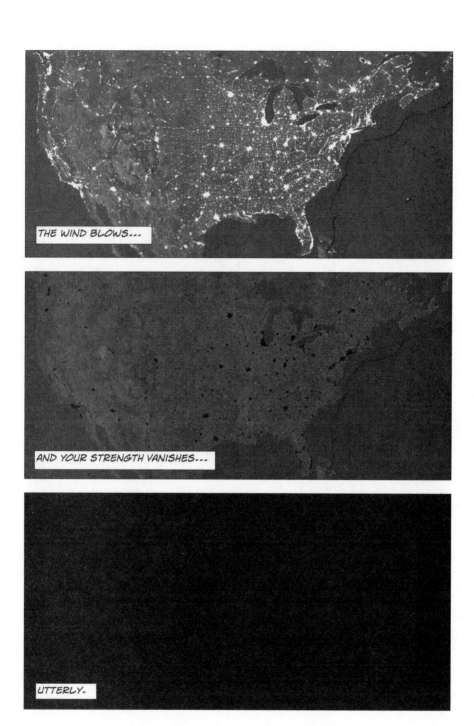

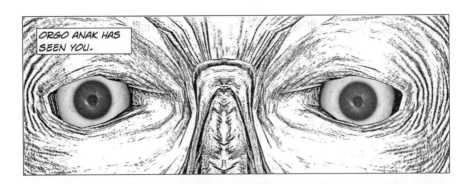

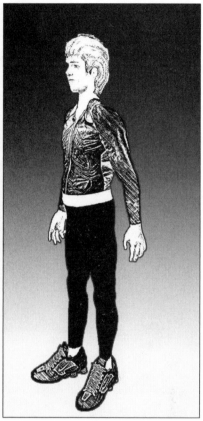
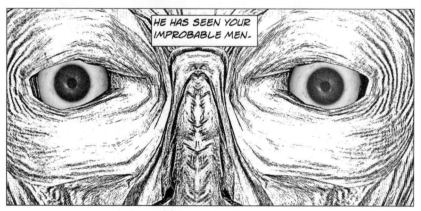

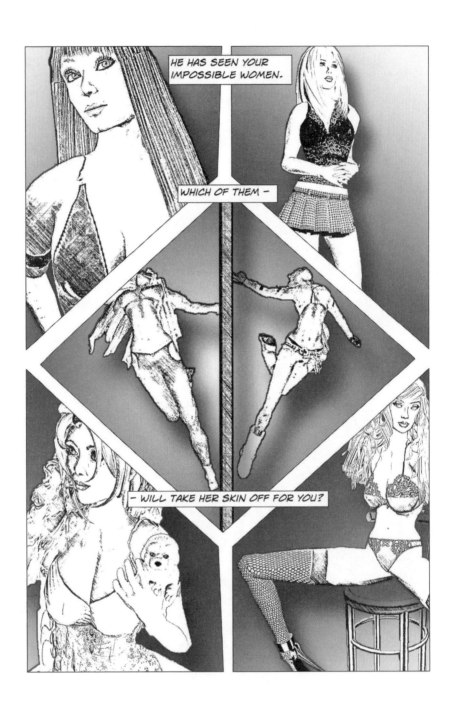

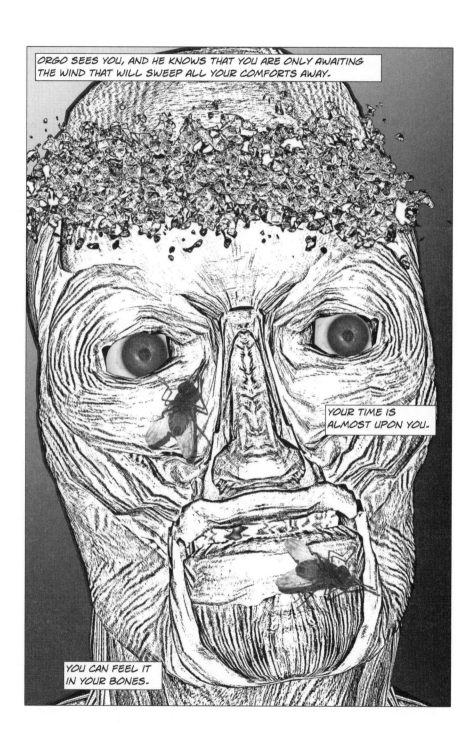

THE GEARS AND WHEELS THAT DRIVE THE FLATLANDS WILL GRIND TO A SLOW AND SHUDDERING HALT.

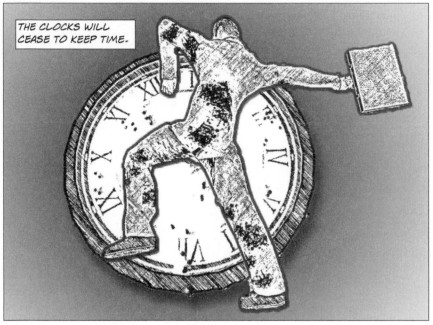

THE CLOCKS WILL CEASE TO KEEP TIME.

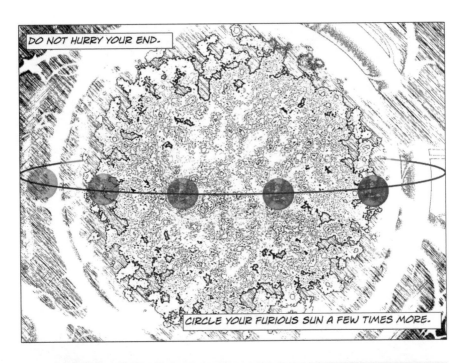

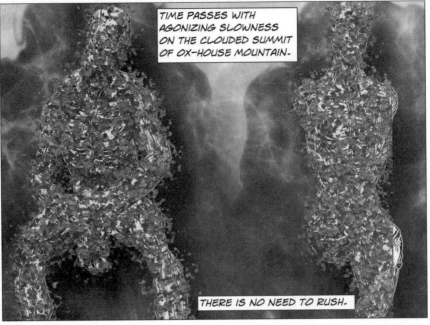

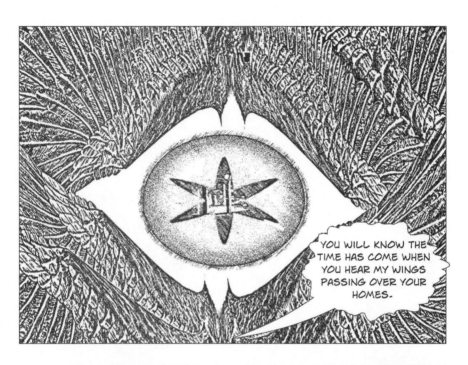

THE BULLHEADED SONS OF ORGO ANAK...

...WILL GET THEIR OWN STRONG SONS...

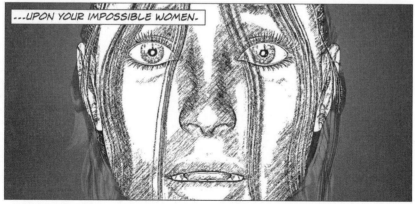

...UPON YOUR IMPOSSIBLE WOMEN.

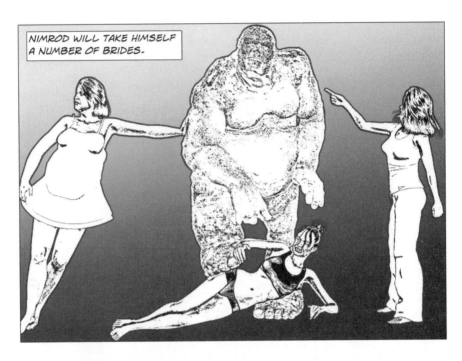

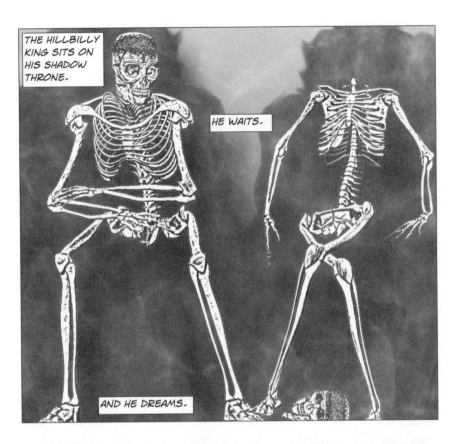

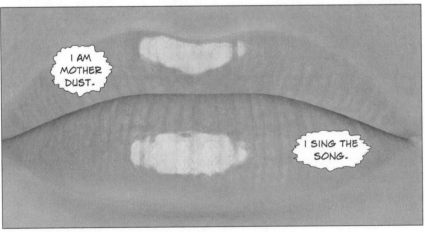

Paula Bohince

Cleaning My Father's House

I've come home, to sit inside this house
among the locusts and the crickets, their goodbye duet,
their chitter and squeak of *So long.*
Packing his things to make room for my own:
his pale blue Easter suit, his Bowie knife, its leather sheath
branded with *Nashville.* Catholic medals,
a finger's-length statue of Christ in agony on the cross.
I touch the open mouth and put Him away.
So much stuff engraved upon a life. His wallet,
like a miniature and battered suitcase, still feels warm.
How can that be? Social Security card
soft as dishcloth, his license, expired now, a laminated
girlie picture behind it—blond barrel curls,
angora sweater unbuttoned.
I find the flannel shirts I gave him one Christmas,
press them to my lips, hungry for his scent of gasoline
and tobacco, pomade and Ivory soap.
Beneath the bed, slippery piles of Stagger Lee and Lena
Horne records, a dozen half-carved
wooden animals. Biographies of Custer, Billy the Kid.
I think my father was a boy, an unhappy child
who played with guns and trouble, who had a daughter
by accident, each of us bewildered by the other.
It's dark outside, end of the longest summer.
We met once, in this life. Even the ash in his ashtray
seems precious, impossible to be rid of.

Heaven

The heifer grazing by her lonesome
has gold in her mouth, and the mark of lightning
on her forehead.

Who doesn't believe in heaven?

Quicksilver thrushes form a chain
in the stable's eaves; the mosquito drags
her spindly legs across the trough,
shivering as lichen catches,
her engine purring in perfect voice.

Even my little pink house, sliding off the hill,
wants to be caught.

The Children

If the wind had been less gutsy
in its unbindings, we'd know them better,
the children

or the afterimage of them,
the teenage couple rapt inside the field
after the rave has died

and dispersed into corn, into cars, into
the trashed curfew.
We'd know them, the two who lay here,

•

ecstasy lowered to ache
and dull grin, glow sticks faded against
colorless weeds.

If the wind had been less federal,
sweeping anew the corn dust, and the clouds
that kept them starry for hours,

now passive against the noon sky:
if only they'd lasted.
If we'd been given more distinct evidence

beyond the condom listing against milkweed, the fox prints, the warmth
of glow sticks in our hands—

neutral again, broken of their magic.
Those dirty pacifiers we suck. Their whistles
we put to mouth and sound.

Dennis Covington

Desire

When my father's people came down from the Appalachians to work in the mills and mines of North Alabama, they brought with them a desire for strong drink, loose women, and visitations by the Holy Ghost. A census taker who interviewed some of these Covingtons noted they were illiterate, and then also checked the box for "deaf, dumb, blind, insane, or idiotic." But it was my grandfather on my mother's side, an ill-tempered railroad detective named Charlie Russell, who kept another woman in Chattanooga and wound up dying of syphilis at the Alabama state mental hospital. I suppose it could be said that desire killed him.

Given that sad history, it's no wonder my mother wanted me to be a doctor and was so disappointed when I didn't become one. But late in life, after her own dementia set in, she called to tell me how proud she was that I had at least become a dentist. Then she asked for an appointment to have her teeth cleaned. I thanked her, but said I'd need to get back with her about that appointment. She'd confused my name, Dennis, with the word *dentist*, and I didn't have the heart to correct her.

Mother's desire on my behalf was more than just a wish or a hope, though. All along, she'd had faith that I'd make something of myself. And faith, the author of Hebrews tells us, is the actual "substance of things hoped for, the evidence of things not seen."

Maybe I am a dentist, and just haven't accepted my calling yet.

At any rate, faith and desire seem to me to be two sides of the same coin. So if faith is the substance of things hoped for, what's desire the substance of? It's a question that defies simple answers.

"Be careful what you wish for," we tell each other.

But with desire, do we really have a choice?

•

On a Friday night in September of 1963, I was fourteen years old and sitting on a band bus in Birmingham, Alabama, after one of our high school football games. A girl named Connie Bieker, a pretty clarinetist who would later become a majorette, sat a few rows ahead of me. She had taken off her band uniform coat and was sticking her arm out the window. The night had been hot, and the bus wasn't air-conditioned. Up ahead there seemed to be a traffic jam. When the bus slowed to a stop, a black youth ran up to the window and slashed Connie's arm with a razor or knife. Hers was not a serious injury, but I still remember the vivid contrast of blood against the sleeve of her white button-down. I remember the rush of desire I felt while looking at that.

The next morning, a young woman named Elizabeth Hood stopped by the Birmingham home of her uncle, Robert Chambliss, a Klansman with a history of racial violence. She told him about the incident on the band bus, the white girl stabbed by a black teenager. She'd read about it in the paper. Chambliss flew into a rage. He told his niece to just wait until Sunday. He said he had enough "stuff" to flatten half of Birmingham.

And that Sunday morning, one of Chambliss's sisters-in-law called her boyfriend, a local sheriff's deputy, and asked him to meet her at their usual rendezvous spot on the outskirts of the city. When the deputy arrived at 8:30, she told him a bomb had been planted at the Sixteenth Street Baptist Church downtown. About two hours later, at 10:22 to be exact, that bomb exploded, killing four black girls who had just arrived for Sunday School. Three of the girls were fourteen years old. Denise McNair, the youngest, was eleven. The sheriff's deputy had been on his way to the church when it happened.

"In those days," he said, many years later, "there were false alarms every time I turned around."

But why had the deputy waited nearly two hours before he got into his car and headed for the church? He said it was a "personal thing" between him and the woman informant.

St. Gregory has warned us that there are holy desires and unholy desires. What makes us think we know the difference?

•

Last summer, for instance, I visited the Dominican Republic in order to get my Spanish back up to speed, and my host family, a woman named Rósula and her four daughters, were more than willing to help. Rósula spoke no English, and although her daughters did to varying degrees, they promised not to on my account. The family's home was in a quiet neighborhood of Santiago de los Caballeros, a city much like the Birmingham of my childhood, except for the courtyard with mango and orange trees; the butterfly orchids that bloomed from the courtyard walls; and the family's parrot Juanita, who shouted ¡Qué rico! when I walked outside to watch the sun rise over the buildings downtown.

Rósula hand-washed all of my clothes, hung them in the courtyard to dry, and prepared delicious meals—plantains, fresh fruit, beans and rice, Creole chicken, seafood stews—more food than I could ever eat, and each meal accompanied by a tropical fruit drink: pineapple, coconut, passion fruit, or tamarind.

A devout Roman Catholic, Rósula also offered me nourishment of a spiritual kind. She taught me to recite the traditional blessing in which God is asked to give "bread to the one who has hunger, and a thirst for justice to those of us who have the bread." She took me to a concert by Sister Glenda, the singing Peruvian nun, and shared her morning devotionals with me from the Spanish edition of *The Upper Room*. When she asked one day what my favorite chapter of the New Testament was—other than the Gospels, of course—I said Hebrews 11, and she recited that first verse about faith, the "substance of things hoped for." Then she added that her favorite chapter was First John 4, the one about love.

Have I mentioned that Rósula was also a dentist? Her office, with its drill and reclining chair, adjoined the living room, and occasionally, when I'd come home from my Spanish lessons, the office door would be open, a patient laid out in the chair, and Rósula's drill could be heard whining over the sound of the soap opera her daughters were watching while Chula, the indoor parrot, ruffled its feathered neck, and the family's teacup chihuahua, Lily, dressed in a dog's ballerina costume, snoozed in one of the girls' laps.

I had two grown daughters myself. Raising them with their mother had been the happiest time of my life. But I'd never been in a house quite like Rósula's, or with a family quite like hers. I started to think I'd stumbled into paradise. And when she emerged from the dental office in her blue tunic and surgical mask, I couldn't help but feel the stirrings of desire, that long ancestral urge toward what we know we cannot have.

The only desire that lasts, my daughter Laura tells me, is the desire for the unattainable. For Truth, as Plato would say. Or for God, Laura adds.

I soon learned that the Dominican Republic, like the South I grew up in, was a landscape haunted by race. In 1937, the dictator Rafael Trujillo ordered the massacre of thousands of black Haitians who had dared to settle there. Trujillo was obsessed with "whitening" the country's population, and even today, although the vast majority of Dominicans come from a mixed racial heritage, one can still find skin whitening creams on the shelves of Santiago pharmaceutical aisles. In addition to the Spanish words *blanco* and *negro*, Dominicans employ a host of other terms to distinguish the intervening shades.

Rósula, for instance, had been the darkest of ten children. And, as I found out at a family wedding in the mountain village of Jarabacoa, her siblings still called her by her childhood nickname: Morena, the dark one. The photograph of Rósula at the age of twelve, on the wall of her parents' living room in Jarabacoa, reminded me of the happy photos I'd once seen of Denise McNair, the eleven-year-old killed in the Birmingham church bombing. Photos from after the bombing were not so easy to look at. They showed Denise stretched out on a coroner's table, a shard of concrete wedged into her brain. It's been nearly fifty years since that awful September morning, but the pertinent facts remain. A desire born of hate and aimed at revenge killed Denise McNair and the other girls. But their deaths could have been prevented were it not for desire of another kind.

When I think of Robert Chambliss, I think of my boyhood Sunday School teacher, who boasted that he was a member of the Klan. I think of my lawyer cousin, Fred Blanton, who helped represent the Klansmen accused of murdering civil rights worker Viola Liuzzo. I think of the Klansmen who picked up a black man near my neighborhood in 1957, took him into the woods and castrated him, pouring turpentine on the open wound before they left him, barely alive, in the trunk of an abandoned car. I think of that newspaper photograph from the Birmingham Trailways bus station on Mother's Day, 1961, the photo of angular white men in shirt sleeves, beating black and white Freedom Riders with iron pipes. I was in the sixth grade at the time, and I was shocked when I recognized, if not the men themselves, then the thing I saw in their faces: the spite and bitter hunger of those poverty-stricken Southern whites who'd come down from the mountains. I suspected even then that I might be one of them.

"You cannot escape history," Abraham Lincoln once said.

But what about desire? Can you ever escape that?

The names of each of Rósula's daughters began with an E: Evelina, Evelyn, Elisa, and Emely. During the terrible reign of Trujillo, there were four other Dominican sisters, the Mirabals, who came of age not far from Santiago. Like Rósula's daughters, they went to Mass and grew up loved and safe. But the Benefactor, as Trujillo called himself, was accustomed to taking young women away from their families to be his concubines. During a ceremonial ball, Minerva Mirabal slapped him when he pressed his groin up against hers. And later, when the sisters became active in the movement to overthrow Trujillo, he ordered the arrest of Minerva and her youngest sister, María Teresa. They were tortured and eventually released, but Trujillo's thugs later ambushed them and their sister Patria on a lonely mountain road and beat them to death.

Throughout their public dissent, the Mirabal sisters had been referred to clandestinely as *Las Mariposas*, The Butterflies, and as word spread of their deaths, images of butterflies—on posters, banners, factory walls—became a means of silent protest against the regime. "Long live The Butterflies!" the protestors cried. Six months later, Trujillo was himself ambushed and shot to death on a beach road south of the capital. Like my Grandfather Russell, a casualty of desire.

One morning, I watched Rósula pick up a pair of heavy kitchen scissors. She was going to cut the wings of Juanita, her outdoor parrot. I'd never seen anyone do something like that, and I must have appeared shocked.

But she explained that otherwise the bird might escape from the cage under the mango tree, and she'd have to scour the neighborhood in hopes of finding and bringing it home.

The parrot struggled, twisted its neck, and pecked at Rósula's hands as she scissored through the stiff flight feathers as though they were nothing more than cloth. But the ordeal was over as quickly as it had begun. Rósula unwrapped the white towel she'd used to restrain the parrot; she eased it back into the cage. And as I watched her deposit the clipped portions of the wings into the garbage, I realized I had witnessed the perfect metaphor for desire—the tragedy of it, the persistence of it. Here I was, a grandfather well into his sixties whose amorous wings had been cut a decade before by cancer surgery too commonplace to name. But still, I was subject to desire.

That afternoon, I told Rósula I intended to write an essay in Spanish. "About what?" she asked.

"Desire."

She was washing dishes at the sink, and she looked over at me skeptically, as if she were calibrating where such a notion might lead.

"It's an essay about the *nature* of desire," I explained. "Like what the author of Hebrews said about the nature of faith."

"Ah," she said. But she wanted to know more, and I'd written nothing but what I thought might be the last two lines, to which she said: "Well, let's hear them, okay?"

So I opened my notebook and read: *Deseo no es la cotorra que estoy buscando en el bosque.* Desire is not the bird that I'm looking for in the forest. *Deseo es el gusano que está comiendo mi corazón.* Desire is the worm that's eating at my heart.

Rósula thought about that a moment, and then toweled off her hands. "But you know what happens to the worm, don't you?"

I shook my head.

"It turns into a butterfly," she said.

On an afternoon toward the end of my stay in Santiago, I was in the backseat of Rósula's car with her oldest daughter, Evelina, while Rósula and a friend of hers from church delivered gifts to a shut-in neighbor.

Evelina and her mother had argued earlier in the day, but things had settled down by then.

"I've never met a woman like your mother," I told her.

Evelina gave me a wry grin. "Yeah, she's crazy. She has plans for you this afternoon."

Plans? My heart leapt. I didn't ask what kind.

And I didn't find out until right before dinner, as I sat on the couch with Lily in my lap. The dog was wearing a bolero and ruffled trousers while we watched a Venezuelan soap opera called *Decisiones*, an episode in which a policeman comes home early to find his wife in bed with his best friend. The policeman has to decide whether or not to pull out his service revolver and shoot them. But during the commercial break, Rósula entered the living room in her blue tunic and surgical mask. She motioned for me to get up and follow her into her dental office. *This is gonna hurt*, I thought.

She adjusted the reclining chair and invited me to make myself comfortable. "Open your mouth," she said. "Wider." And she examined my teeth, tapping each one with her pointed probe. When she got to an upper right bicuspid, she tapped it two or three more times and said, "How long have you had this filling?"

"I don't know. Since I was a teenager, I guess."

"I thought so. We don't use fillings like this anymore. It's black. It's ugly. I'm going to take it out and put in one that's whiter. Do you have problems with your heart?"

Did I have problems with my heart?

I thought about my mother, whom I'd never loved the way I should have. I thought about the women I'd desired but never truly loved, the women I'd left who'd loved me, the women I'd loved who'd left me. I thought about the two marriages that had ended in divorce. I thought about the children their mother and I had prayed we'd be able to have, and about the child before them that we'd aborted. I thought about the difference between faith and desire. If faith was the substance of the things we'd hoped for, then desire was the substance of the things we'd lost. Desire was not the bird I was looking for in the forest. Desire was the worm that was eating at my heart.

Rósula lifted her surgical mask. "Dennis, did you hear me? I asked if you had problems with your heart."

I said, "No, I don't think so."

"Good, because I'm going to give you an anesthetic." She readjusted her mask. And then she shot me up with Novocain and cranked up her ancient drill.

Jeff Mann

715 Willey Street

It betrays my country roots, how awed I am by this sight, a city steaming and gleaming in the rain. Chance or my host's careful choice, I'm not sure which, but this Northern Kentucky hotel room must be the best in the house. It's set high within tonight's storm, overlooking the Ohio River and facing Cincinnati's riverfront, a complexity of bridges, interstates, and glowing office buildings. The scene's dramatic; the view's a privilege. I almost feel as if I've arrived, as if this is some fancy hotel room reserved for rock stars or visiting royalty.

No real star here. I've come to Northern Kentucky University at the kind request of a man who's teaching my new book, *Loving Mountains, Loving Men,* in his grad class on Appalachian Literature. I've spoken to his students and given a reading. His department has paid for this hotel room. I don't get a lot of these invitations—writing about gay people in Appalachia doesn't net me much money or attention—so it's nice to feel successful for an evening.

As exhilarating as the attention has been, I'm tired after the long day of driving, speaking, and then chatting with folks at the post-reading party. I'm glad to be alone now, happy to sit by this big window in the dark and watch the city glitter in the rain. The bed's king-sized—enough room for me and a couple of country-music stars, preferably Tim McGraw and Chris Cagle—but they're inconveniently not here, and I'm too exhausted to do more than cuddle anyway.

Lights in the river: like phosphorescent watercolors, yellow and blue, swirled over a black canvas. Cities: beautiful from a distance, a delight to visit, but I can't imagine living in one. I'm too addicted to solitude and silence, which this hotel room is at present providing. "Chris, Tim, time for bed!" I say, grinning at the foolish impossibility of fancy, heading to the bathroom to brush my teeth. I'm in my late forties: the same decades that have allowed me a small literary reputation have diminished my erotic opportunities and, in consequence, deepened my fantasy life. Thus, these days, Tim and Chris are my houseboys. They don't get much cleaning and cooking done since they spend most of the time shirtless, struggling, sweaty, gagged, and bound back to back in my basement. Plus imaginary slaves aren't good dishwashers to begin with.

I'm lying in bed naked, relishing interior fantasy, exterior warmth and quiet, watching the veils of rain diminish, when it hits me.

Cincinnati. Cincinnati.

Last I heard, Allen was living here. Is he still here? Is he even alive? When you don't hear from a college friend for years, if you're a gay man of my generation, you can't help but worry and wonder about the worst.

The phonebook's huge, like most cities'. It takes me a while to find what I'm looking for, but there the name is. He's still on earth. It's not too late, so I call. Machine, not man. But for the first time in fifteen years I hear his voice. I speak into the phone, and somewhere my words are seized by magnetic tape on his answering machine. By this room I will leave tomorrow and never see again, the Ohio River runs, making small sounds not audible at this distance. Across its rain-stippled black back, restless as history, the city lights spill their aspirations.

Everyone called it Augie's, after the owner. The official name was the Washington Café, at the bottom of Walnut Street, near the Monongahela River. Seedy and friendly, like most gay hangouts outside large urban areas, with a low bar along one wall, a line of wooden booths along the other. Now it's a small art gallery, but for a few years in the late 1970s it was the only gay bar in Morgantown, West Virginia. It was the first gay bar I ever entered, age seventeen, the spring of 1977. With only a couple more months of high school to endure before I graduated, I was getting an advance taste of freedom and university life by visiting my lesbian buddy Carolyn, a hometown friend who was attending West Virginia University. She figured it was time for me to glimpse some gay nightlife, so down to Augie's we went. I was excited to be in Queer Space for the first time, and scared too, afraid a horde of homophobes wielding baseball bats might burst in any second. Natural introvert, small-town boy in the city, I sat in a booth with Carolyn, listened to Joni Mitchell on the tiny table jukebox, and watched wide-eyed. I had never seen so many gays and lesbians in one room before.

Carolyn introduced me to several folks that night who would later become enduring friends of mine, and Allen was one of them. The son of a coal miner, Allen had, like me, grown up in southern West Virginia, in Raleigh County, which adjoins my home county of Summers. He was tall and lean, with short, wavy light-brown hair, a handsome, angular face, and large strong hands. It took me only that first evening to discover that he had the kind of quick, mercurial, wicked wit that so many gay men possess, a sharp intelligence I can never match, bulky Caliban that I am, but which I wholeheartedly savor. His whispered comments about this and that bar patron would have done Oscar Wilde proud.

Acerbic he could certainly be, but he was also kind. That evening, he did his best to make me, shy, unsure, shaggy-haired kid that I was, feel at ease. There was, to begin with, no major erotic chemistry between us, which allowed us to skip the complications of sexual attraction and move right into a simpler friendship. Immature men have real problems mixing erotic and platonic love—fucking a friend can ruin the relationship—but we were to be spared those dangers, for the most part.

When, in August 1977, I began my studies at West Virginia University, he and Carolyn were sharing an apartment in a broken-down old house in Sunnyside, Morgantown's student ghetto. I was living in Boreman Hall, a brick dorm on the Downtown Campus, with a clodlike roommate from Greenbrier County who decorated the walls with *Penthouse* pinups and did laundry at two in the morning. I've never been particularly patient, I've always cherished privacy, not to mention uninterrupted sleep, and, besides, I'd come to college not only to get an education, but to spend time with other queers, so it wasn't long before I was sleeping most nights on the lumpy couch in Allen and Carolyn's University Avenue apartment. (*How did I stand it?* I wincingly ask myself at age forty-seven. The answer: an eighteen-year-old back.)

Carolyn I'd gone to high school with. Allen I had only begun to know. Nevertheless, he never complained about my regular presence in their apartment. On the contrary. In I'd stump, rain beading on my leather jacket and in my sparse beard, and there he'd be, smoking and studying by the window or hunched over his sketchpad creating another amazing image with ink or watercolor. Far more cognizant of the gay world than I—in fact, more competent and knowledgeable in just about everything—Allen took me under his wing. He told me about gay bar etiquette, the fine points of cruising, the ins and outs of oral and anal sex. I hardly knew how to make instant coffee—I'd been spoiled by the good cooks in my family but had as yet learned none of their skills—but Allen was an old hand in the kitchen. He cooked us stews, baked macaroni and cheese, on snowy nights whipped up the Unofficial West Virginia State Dish—brown beans and cornbread. We played Joni Mitchell, Janis Ian, and David Bowie into the wee hours, sitting at the little kitchen table studying side by side: his Sociology and Costume Design, my British Lit and Aesthetics. With Carolyn, Laura, Cin, and other lesbian friends, we'd bustle into the Fox—the latest gay watering hole now that Augie had died and the Washington Café had closed—where Allen would advise me on alcohol options like Tequila Sunrises and Harvey Wallbangers (a far cry from the neat Scotch I favor today) and coach my uncoordinated body in the various bump-and-grind dance moves appropriate to the thumping music of Donna Summer and the Village People. I had never danced with a man before, but Allen was a patient teacher.

We had our hard times. From this distance, both the pleasures and the adversities of college days seem unnaturally vivid, as if I stand in the gentle hills of the Piedmont looking back on a sheer mountain landscape I've recently passed through successfully but with some effort, a world far more dramatic and more difficult to traverse than the one I inhabit now. One night we returned to Allen's apartment to discover that someone had broken in and taken the few things of value. Another time, an anonymous someone called to mutter homophobic threats. Once, during that savage winter of '77–'78, when snow layered the ground in November and stubbornly remained, with regular supplements from the sky, till March, when I was constantly being hailed by complete strangers to help them push their wheel-churning cars out of drifts, the heat in Allen's apartment failed for 48 hours and we ended up sleeping together in a completely unerotic attempt to avoid freezing to death.

At the end of my first semester, Carolyn quit school and moved out; a charmer named Larry moved in, stayed a few months, then decamped to Florida with Allen's best blazer, leaving behind an enormous long-distance phone bill Allen ended up having to pay. I developed a huge infatuation with one of Allen's friends, Bob, a handsome and thoroughly superficial Italian-American guy from Weston, was far too shy to make my interest known, and then one night lay in agony on the couch listening to Allen and Bob make drunken, noisy love in the adjoining bedroom. I didn't speak to Allen for a few weeks after that.

Despite minor conflicts, we decided to become roommates, for I was hot to escape dorm life. By the beginning of my sophomore year, Allen and I were sharing the second-floor apartment at 715 Willey Street. That address now, as resonant for me as Proust's madeleine, evokes futile nostalgia, a clichéd longing for the Lost Abode of Youth in which those middle-aged tend to indulge. During my brief returns to Morgantown, I sometimes drive past that house, and its present decrepitude reminds me both of the relative rapidity with which all I know and love is gradually leaving this earth and of that circle of friends—Allen, Laura, Cin, Kaye—who helped me survive my youthful despair, sexual frustration, and loneliness.

Odd what returns to me, almost thirty years later, poised here over my keyboard. I live in Virginia now, with John, my partner of ten years, in Pulaski, a small mountain town very much like the ones I grew up in. I'm publishing books, teaching university students. My beard and chest hair are full of gray, and just lately I have started to notice that same silvery glitter in the fur on my forearms. I have several gay acquaintances, not one truly close gay male friend. I haven't seen Allen in almost twenty years. Still, typing this, I find my way back.

Allen is preparing Cornish game hens, the first I've had. But before they're baked, the hens must dance. Allen's whimsical humor so often pulls me from my depressions. One minute I'm lying in front of our gas fireplace brooding over my celibacy and the cursed and unerring accuracy with which I desire men who have no desire for me, and the next, at Allen's suggestion, we are dangling the hens by their little wings and propelling them in a complex pas de deux across the kitchen table. They bow, they leap, they circle like passionate partners, the Ballet of the Dwarf-Fowl. Allen and I laugh till we hurt.

I'm sitting at the kitchen table making index cards to help me memorize dendrology facts more efficiently—maples have opposite leaves, black walnut leaf scars look like clown faces—when Allen, in one of his frequent prankish moods, slips up behind me. He gently hooks my nostrils with two fingers, pulls my face up and back while I grin and cuss, admires the piggy-nose configuration he's created, says "Oink, Oink, Pussy-Face!" then lets loose and bounds beyond the reach of my play-punch. Ever since my beard has started to fill in, he calls me Pussy Face. He also has elaborate jokes about how much I supposedly love to rim German Shepherds. We're boys from small towns in southern West Virginia: rank humor is par for the course.

"Oh Gawd, it's the Dana and Kaye Show!" I whisper, sticking my head into Allen's overheated bedroom. He's always turning the little heater in his room up and then sleeping under nothing but a sheet, even in the bitter winter weather. I drag him into my bedroom, where the window's cracked a bit even in January and quilts are heaped in layers upon the rarely washed sheets. "Now listen!" I urge, handing him the glass. He puts it to the bare wood floor, listens a minute, and grins. Even without the aid of the glass, I can make out "Oh . . . my . . . God . . . Dana!" Lesbian lovemaking at its loudest. "We should invite folks in and charge for this!" I say, eager entrepreneur.

Allen's driving us back from Frostburg, Maryland, where we've dropped off Lisa, a lesbian friend. While there, Lisa's cronies coaxed me into trying my first bong. Pot is something I've smoked socially, but it's never really hit me before. Now, sitting in the passenger seat and watching the purple-gray mountains stream by, I'm so fucking high I hardly know where I am. It's scary as hell, though I try to act calm, fight back the panic, and just listen to the tape Allen's got playing. It's at this point in my chemical confusion that a helicopter appears in silhouette against the sunset's red West. Lord God, I think, am I hallucinating? Was there angel dust in that weed? Is my mind screwed up for good? As casually as I can, I say, "Uh, man, look at that. Uh, what, uh. . . ?" I'm afraid to say, "Look, is that a helicopter?" because I'm half-convinced that he isn't seeing what I'm seeing, which would mean that my brain is ruined and I'll be trapped in Semi-Rutabagahood for the rest of my life. Allen says, "That's a sweet chariot come for to carry you home, you hopped-up cocksucker!" I choke, he laughs and pats my thigh. "Take a nap, Jeff," he says, and I do.

It's a windy April evening. We've been listening to the house creak, sprawling on the floor in front of the gas fire, indulging in what is very expensive beer to students as poor as we are, the rare elixir Michelob (which, in my much later beer-snob days, I'll describe as a product that "ain't fit to douche a dog"). We're telling ghost stories—I have the drowned lady who haunts Bluestone Reservoir, he's got some kind of mine-disaster specter. "Well, I'm hitting the sack," says Allen, just about the time I'm thoroughly creeped out. "Sweet dreams," he says wickedly, closing his bedroom door. Trying to relax, I piddle around ineptly on my new guitar—Joni Mitchell's exotic tunings are challenging for a novice—then head for bed myself.

Shucking off my clothes, I slip between grimy sheets. I lie there in the dark, thinking about mine ghosts and monsters. The wind rattling the window screen right beside my bed isn't helping, so I grab a Kleenex, close my eyes, and start constructing a detailed fantasy about the beefy black-bearded boy I heartily and hopelessly covet in dendrology class. I've got a rag tied between the stud's teeth, his hands roped behind his back, and am lapping his hairy beer belly when something scratches the screen. I start, drop my dick, stare into the darkness. The scratching continues—I'm seeing four-inch-long claws—then a sinister something rasps, "Jefffff . . ." Suddenly the screen rattles and a white face is pressed against the window.

"Holy fuck!!" I shout, leaping out of bed with a rapidly declining hard-on just about the time laughter starts rolling through the screen. It's that bastard Allen. He's climbed out of his bedroom window onto the top of the porch roof and crawled over to my window, all to see if he can make me piss myself. By the time he climbs back in, I'm poised to tackle him. We roll around for a

while, laughing and cussing, before he pins me down. I'm the bearded, butch, aspiring leatherman, but he's always the one who wins our wrestling matches. He's always been stronger.

Allen graduated at the end of that year. We parted uneasily. I was self-ish and dominating, he was tired of catering to me, he said. I found other accommodations, with a rule-bound recluse I took to calling the Sterile Cuckoo. After a few months of his obsessive-compulsive behavior, I moved into a shabby two-room place on Falling Run Road and began what was to be a long series of years of living alone. Mutual friends informed me that Allen's social-work degree wasn't of much use in the work world, and pretty soon I heard that he was living with his Aunt Lil near Beckley and working in a tollbooth on the West Virginia Turnpike.

We reestablished contact fast—rural Appalachia is a fairly hostile environment, so gay boys there need to stick together. Soon, during my summers home in Hinton, I would spend a weekend every now and then in Stanaford, the Beckley suburb where he'd grown up and where his parents and aunt still lived. Allen and I would drive an hour down the West Virginia Turnpike to Charleston, the state capital, and the Grand Palace, a gay bar of many years' duration, to gyrate on the check-erboard of the dance floor, an elevated structure lit from within, to drink cheap beer, and to watch the big-haired drag queens cavort. As usual, Allen flirted with ease, while I avoided the guys I found attractive, far too insecure to introduce myself, much less ask them to dance. Allen, bless him, saved every other dance for me.

Worn-out with hours of disco, we'd face a 2 A.M. drive through the dark mountains of Kanawha, Fayette, and Raleigh Counties back to Stanaford. (We gay folks in rural regions will drive a long way for some precious time with Our Kind.) We'd sleep together—only once did cuddling lead to more, a quiet coupling with his aunt snoring in the next room, a little 69ing that left minimal morning-after awkwardness and was never spoken of afterwards. Put two young and perpetually horny gay men in a bed, and something's bound to happen sooner or later. From the perspective of middle age, I would say that's reason not for judgment but for celebration. Even in my twenties, the concept of *carpe diem* made perfect sense to me.

Then those late-morning breakfasts courtesy of Mizz Lil, biscuits with sausage gravy made not from milk but water, along with eggs, juice, and lots and lots of coffee. Most folks from my neck of the woods, however modest their means, are superbly hospitable, and I soon learned where Allen had inherited his culinary skills. Nights we didn't drive to Charleston would be composed of stiff drinks and big meals, TV and gossip. Breathless as a Tennessee Williams heroine, Lil would tell tale after tale. Once she gasped, "I took my prescription to the drugstore, and, Lord God, it cost me fifty dollars for four pills. 'Fifty dollars for four pills!?' I said, 'I swan, I'm going to the liquor store, I'm going to buy a bottle of rum, I'm going to go home and have a rum and coke, I'm going to have a rum and coke if it hairlips the president!' I did, I said, 'Fifty dollars for four pills. . . . I'm going to have me a rum and coke and I don't care if it hairlips the president!' Indeed I did, I said..." When, years later, I read Florence King's *Confessions of a Failed Southern Lady* in which she claims that many Southern women feel compelled to say things three times, I could only grin at the familiar rhetorical pattern.

How did Allen and I drift apart? I finished undergraduate school, then graduate school, lived in Washington, DC, for a bleak and lonely semester, returned to West Virginia, and began teaching as an overworked and poorly paid instructor in the English Department at WVU. Allen saved his turnpike money and then returned to WVU for a degree in art. He settled down with a new lover, McCarty, in a Tudor-style house not far from my apartment. There we were in Morgantown again, but both so busy there was little time together. He took me down into the bowels of the mazelike Creative Arts Center a few times to show me his sculpture studio, and I attended his senior exhibit. After years of painting, he was focusing on sculptures now, creating disturbing constructs that often evoked the AIDS crisis—slate-gray boxes with shards of mirror and dangling bones. One he gave me, and it stood ominously in my living room until I moved to Blacksburg in 1989. It was too large to take with me; I gave it to McCarty. Their relationship had apparently been provisional from the first—Allen knew he'd be leaving, going to grad school—so McCarty was left with an apartment full of Allen's paintings and sculptures, while Allen moved on to Cincinnati about the time I got a new job at Virginia Tech.

How did we lose touch so completely? Both of us had new lives, in towns far apart. Neither was good at steady correspondence. I made a new set of friends in Blacksburg, fell wildly in love with a man already partnered, grieved terribly when he and his lover left town, then, desperate for consolation, slept around as much as possible. Eventually I met John, my present partner. Eventually I got a postcard announcing an art show of Allen's in Cincinnati. In 1998, I sent him a copy of *Bliss*, my first poetry chapbook, but heard nothing back. Allen had always been the kind of independent friend who waited for invitations from others to jaunt out together but rarely initiated contact himself. I'm the proud sort who thinks, "Now it's *your* turn to get hold of *me*." I construct little tests for people, count things up, brood over tit for tat. Bad combination. "Well, fuck this," I thought, hoping for and never receiving a note from him gushing over the quality of my poetry. Laura and Kaye, when I saw them during vacation visits, always asked me about him but had never heard from him either. He'd moved to Ohio and simply vanished. "Well, that's what comes from living in the Midwest," I growled, more devoted to my mountains than ever.

Why have I had so few gay male friendships? I wonder this a lot in my middle years. I've had many good lesbian friends, quite a few good straight friends, but almost no close gay friends. There was James, someone I met through Larry, the handsome liar who'd left Allen with that unpaid phone bill so long ago. James and I had an on-again/off-again friendship for two decades. I envied him his string of desirable butch-bottom lovers, and he relished my envy, as well as the way my solitary charmlessness, like leaden foil, accentuated his gemlike charisma. Fallings out, years without contact, reconciliations . . . until, in Rehoboth Beach in the late nineties, over the pettiest of reasons, one estrangement finally took. More recently, there was David, who kept his careful distance at the same time that he relished my cocktails and I relished his eminently quotable wit. He left town recently, and he was palpably chilly to me at our last meeting, for reasons I have yet to discern. My only present gay male friends are Dan and Phil, though the relationship is long-distance now that John and I have moved to Pulaski. We share weekends of martinis and manhattans, comfort food, and Netflix two or three times a year.

Am I too rural in my values to appreciate or be appreciated by most other gay men, who are largely urban and urbane? Am I too somber, the dark poet who stands in the corner brooding amidst the glittering party chatter? Too self-consciously butch, the token leatherbear, the bearded BDSM guy who makes the vanilla types nervous? I don't want to talk about home appliances, the Tony Awards, or *Project Runway*. I want to talk about mythology, country music, poetry, guitars, and pickup trucks.

Ah, too late to change. This ole dawg needs no new tricks. I have John, I have family, I have my work, I have sufficient friends old and new. Still, I look backward as often as I look forward, for the years behind begin to outnumber the years likely to come. I want those friends of my youth to know how much their help meant at that crucial point in my development. I want, if possible, to see them all again, faces creased by the same decades that have creased mine. Thus, after years without contact, that phone call I made from a Northern Kentucky hotel room, overlooking the subtle and ceaseless black flow of the Ohio.

Here's that phone call's answer, one evening a month later, here in Pulaski, with Hilda, our one local queer friend, over for dinner. I'm warm on Irish whiskey, we're all three full from another of my big, fattening country meals, relaxing in the living room, watching the cats chase one another, when the phone rings. It's Allen. He's using the phone number I left on his answering machine. Amazed, I carry the phone into the dark library and sprawl on the couch for a good twenty minutes, laughing, catching up, reminiscing, before John appears at the door, annoyed, pointing out what a bad host I'm being. "It's Allen, dammit!"—I'm a specialist in the subtle snarl—"You've heard me talk about Allen. I haven't seen him in fifteen years!" John cocks an eyebrow—he's a specialist at tacit disapproval—and returns to keep Hilda company.

I'm too Southern not to get off the phone fast—bad manners are indeed the ultimate accusation—but I've heard what I need to know. Allen's still sculpting in Cincinnati, piecing together a living at this and that (as artists often must), as healthy and vigorous and witty as ever. We agree that it's been too long, that we must set up a meeting soon. What's unspoken is that we're both approaching fifty. The time that might allow for reunions is dwindling fast.

An interviewer once asked me what I missed most from my gay youth, and I replied, with only a little hesitation, "Dancing." I left behind my dancing days in 1989, when I moved from Morgantown, with its conveniently located downtown gay bar, to Blacksburg, where the nearest gay bar is in Roanoke, a forty-five-minute drive away. Living now in Pulaski, I only get to gay bars when John and I travel, to DC, San Francisco, New Orleans, and those bars are almost always bear or leather bars, where there's little to no dancing. I guess it's thought not butch enough.

I have a trifling secret. My partner doesn't know this yet, but I'll share it with you. When I lift weights in our basement—the Radon Gym, I call it, since the radon test results were declared "inconclusive"—in between sets, I shadowbox and dance. I always play loud music when I lift, usually Melissa Etheridge, and most songs have sufficient beat for me to move to. There I am, a beefy, silver-bearded, bald leatherbear in wife-beater, camo shorts, and weightlifting gloves, an overgrown boy with pumped-up hairy chest, tattooed arms, and a sheepish grin. I twitch my hips, hump the darkness, and punch the air, my only partner/rival/lover the wide-shouldered shadow moving along the wall. The few boxing moves I learned a while back at the Virginia Tech Boxing Club; the few dance moves are those same ones Allen taught me long years ago, when I was so young, so ignorant, so innocent, and so in need of the guidance he gave me. I never could master the complex disco steps at which Allen was so adept. He was always the better dancer.

Maurice Manning

Culture

Some of us in cahoots with the birds
are smiling, silly smiles, because
the sun in the barn lot is warmer
today and that means nothing in
particular, but it is a change.
Someone, my neighbor's neighbor over
the hill, shears sheep and helps
with lambing. Beech Fork, the river,
is named for a tree and in a way
that's a symbol and also an idea;
we have a grove, we have a stand.
We like to be quiet and have our thoughts;
we remember the old piano teacher,
her spinet, an instrument that came
to town on a railroad car
and went by mule and wagon a ways
to the old brick house. We talk,
we graft the apple branch and wait
another season for the fruit;
we have a church house here, it's one
big room, we have a hummingbird
with a silver shiny greenish throat.

Provincial Thought

We get things in our head, a sort
of wonder I suppose, a notion,
about where to stand on the hill to see
the white blur of a steeple eight
or maybe ten miles away
at the center of a country town
whose school has been consolidated,
and the little country store, where news
and gossip spread around and maybe
a local discovery was claimed
by one of the loafers there, is closed.
Going to find that spot on the hill
in order to see from a certain prospect
a world far enough away it seems
a symbol is a walk that brings
an important silence down on us.
You could say, I guess, it makes us think—
just walking up a hill to find
a part in the distance that looks familiar.
It makes me think that walking in silence
and going up to where the woods
have made an agreement to leave
an opening—that walk has become
a plain responsibility.
Yet it seems to be a kind of freedom.
One time, a pretty good while back,
I was walking up the little hill
early in the spring before
the leaves had laced the trees together,
and I looked down the hollow and saw
a solitary splay of white,

an early patch of dogwood blossom.
It looked farther away than it was;
it struck me as a symbol inside
another symbol, a silence inside
a silence, and another silence fell
on me. The blossom patch was strange,
but it reminded me of something—
an old woman's puff of breath,
or a white shadow, or maybe both.
It has seemed too much to think about,
an abundance too great for words
or the slower motions of my mind,
and that itself is now a thought,
lodged in a place of its own across
from a hill and in between a distance
of other hills and things unseen—
I've kept it there, and I will keep it,
from loyalty or sentiment
it doesn't matter, I'm keeping it.

The Geography of Yonder

So living under one hill
and at the foot of another leaves
the daylight pinched by morning
and pinched again when the sun declines
behind the other higher hill—
yet the farther face of both receives
its only glow when evening stills
the deeper woods with its slow approach
and the sky is closing like an eye
whose lid is lowered down with sleep.

This is how my people lived,
with inclination at their feet,
where the land is round and mildly peaked
and made to have two sides.
Always we behold the two,
this side and then the yonder one;
what happens on the one reaches
the other in different form, like a dream,
or a memory faint in its recollection—
which itself in time becomes a dream—
and the dream illuminates the real
remaining forms of hills and trees
and the chalk-white path of the stream
which seems to have no age, no sign
of its beginning save at its head,
where water quietly appears
like a voice. I imagine a boy came up
this stream at the idle end of summer
some years ago, and walking and knowing
he was becoming part of himself
before he had the vocabulary
for being, he noticed he was dreaming,
and suddenly he learned the trick
of gloomy amazement that the woods
are God's idea, the living dream
with nothing as its precedent.
So he went back and came to know
that place, and imagined those before
who knew the place before and those
who knew it first, and knowing the past
and loving the people he never knew
who lived between the two hills,
he came to know himself and knew
he was a necessary part
of the continuity and that

continuation, all along,
was at once the idea and its meaning.
I now believe that boy was me,
without philosophy, without
a thought that wasn't handed down.
And then I saw another form
that seemed to run beside the stream,
the remnant of a stone wall
discovered in the woods where someone
had laid it for a purpose now
unknown. Briefly the wall and the stream
are parallel, but the older form
has long outlasted the latter; once
a day and at the end of the day
the two are visible together,
as if two gods took turns and one
gave out, and that makes dreaming here
in this slow, unpeopled place a sad
and necessary thing to do,
because the idea is to keep
the first idea and follow it.
This is the story, the story I've learned
two ways to tell myself, the two
uncertain ways to figure heaven,
and I'm inclined to believe them both.

Vagina Dentata

I have twenty-eight teeth, which is normal for my age, perhaps. I'm bicycling between appointments, one windy October day. Polar visits of personal significance, between which I alternate.

This is a landmark interrogation of each end of me. For someone who avoids the annual visits, to do them both in the same day seems perverse. Masochistic.

My dentist is a sweet girl, who sometimes appears cross-eyed. I wonder if she huffs the nitrous oxide on slow days, what we used to jokingly term "hippie crack."

It was *that* good. Euphoria, deep voice (OHHHHHH YEAHHHHH), and then melting into the chair. But it was costly and hard to find, undoubtedly stolen, with headaches after.

Coveted bottles of Reddi-Whip™ in the absence of tanks. More authoritatively, as William James reported in an 1882 essay: ". . . only as sobriety returns, the feeling of insight fades."

And then, knowingly: ". . . and one is left staring vacantly at a few disjointed phrases, as one stares at a cadaverous-looking snow-peak from which sunset glow has just fled."

Or my favorite quote from that same essay (literally) on laughing gas: "There are no differences but differences of degree between different degrees of difference and no difference."

No one thinks about the impending despair when in the midst of joy. We should know better. The balance due is always taken by time eventually, seconds draining.

Counting relaxes me ... just one needle today. She rubs my gum, counting ... seven ... eight ... releasing on nine ...

My fourteen teeth, upper and lower. Humans are said to have only nine orifices despite the duplicitous mouth. Nine is a holy number. Except women have one more.

Maybe we don't count so closely, or that extra is too shameful, or holier than holy, or maybe we only count men, so obviously nearer to God's math.

(Surely He has twenty-eight teeth.) But our wisdom teeth ... Do we count removals? Phantom teeth, rogue gall bladders, cancer-ridden or cyst-knotted wombs ...

While the dentist works, I think about that morning. Reflection is impossible in the moment, without hindsight—this we know—but it always feels present when remembering.

My pap is routine, but not yearly for me. Back home in Appalachia I never went to the doctor until something desperate was required. Checkups were too expensive.

With good insurance now, next door to the hospital campus, I go. I'm told to undress. They have a cabinet for my clothes. The gown ...

The seamless babble of nervousness and worry, overall that is "normal," she says. The pressure, the ceiling, a subtle probe, warm smile, then an uncomfortable cervical scrape.

•

But it is over, the visit and the passage, just in case I abuse the tense. The letter has come, with one box checked. No follow-up needed *exactly*.

One year later she will tell me what this means, unless I call her today: "Atypical squamous cells of undetermined significance." Of course I call, and am told:

"We often see these. We don't worry unless they come back this way twice in a row. They didn't seem precancerous. Insurance companies don't like . . ."

I know about insurance companies. While I look for my pap results, I sift through stacks of dental paperwork. I've been to the dentist eight times this fall.

Unbearable pain, x-rays, root canal, scaling quadrant one, scaling two through four, fitting for temporary crown, placing of the permanent crown, two fillings, two more. Because of negligence.

Time turns me again. I'm in the chair, my tongue wheeling around the nub that will wear a temporary resin crown for three weeks. I was not prepared.

In a mirror, my dentist showed me the "dead" tooth, which the endodontist had defended: "It still serves a purpose. We don't dismiss citizens who are so functional."

Perhaps in his country, even the dead serve. (Chilling thought.) In hillbilly nonchalance, I had almost ordered this tooth extracted. The cost of keeping it had seemed exorbitant.

But dental myths had overwhelmed me: "Your bottom tooth will grow upward to fill the empty space," or more likely, "Your teeth will shift." This much I believed.

•

Still, I have not seen a single picture of what I mockingly term the "dental fang," nor did I in my pain-ridden state care for one lone bicuspid.

But if there is one certain memory, it is jogged by looking at my peg-tooth in the mirror: I had insisted. There it was—a stub of my skull.

This is what they mean by the morbid phrase "we knew her by her dental records." With all the gravitas of private history, one deeper trauma was stirred:

Of seeing in the moments after falling on my face into carpeted concrete the smear of my mouth, two centrals gone. I must have been four or five.

Because the deciduous (baby) teeth lay the groundwork for the oral cavity, and prepare the space for the later permanents, oversized premature buckteeth were mine for many years.

Which was the greater trauma? Of loss, bullying, or endless orthodontic visits? A single autumn of dental appointments cannot compare to what was for me, then, perfect torture.

A head-brace, so obvious, and nearly as humiliating as my rabbity overbite had been. And years of nightmares wherein I would lose my teeth; they'd all tumble free.

Once, in rare intimacy between strangers, my ex-husband was asked what happened in his best dreams, by a mountain man who quite conspicuously was missing half his teeth.

My ex answered, unself-consciously, "The sun is shining and I have all my teeth." (Changing the subject can divert awareness of a faux pas, however low the magnitude.)

I wonder if I can still say I have "all my teeth." When the day arrived for my permanent porcelain crown to be fitted, I was carefully warned:

"Chewing ice will break your crown." I had not wondered in a long time whether such Freudian fixations were luxuries I maintained anymore. Days later I caught myself.

My uncle had all of his teeth removed in his fifties to cheat his greedy dentist of a soft retirement, or so he says. He is somewhat mistrustful.

Shuffling responsibility is what we're best at. We're midwives to our own resentments. We "give birth astride a grave," to paraphrase Beckett's Pozzo, "then it's night once more."

Bringing to light our failings, attributing culpability, is what keeps lawyers and psychologists in business. The two disciplines are inextricably linked, says psychoanalyst, essayist, and critic Adam Phillips.

In my own peculiar associations, I link dentists to gynecologists. They best understand their clients' reluctance to visit; are similarly in care of a private (and provocative) darkness.

The dentist is guardian of a number of teeth, our gums, our innocent pretensions to sterile whiteness. The other assumes care of our southerly pleasure, our regenerative functions.

Only three to four hundred human eggs follow us into maturity, I recall, though I hesitate to read my expiring anxieties as merely the ticks of a biological clock.

My worry is not over having more children. I'm concerned that my body has changed without my noticing, as if we already have too many secrets between us.

For instance, I don't remember myself appearing (during infrequent and hesitant self-inspection) this way, but am reassured by my doctor that childbirth is traumatic, that the vagina scars.

Or, I think back to times when I was married, when I sometimes made love grudgingly: from duty, out of guilt, without desire, miserably, in isolation, often painfully.

Did I damage myself? Still, I am "normal." There is, in my yet-unwritten *kama sutra*, a pleasurable effect of scarring, and lovers who enjoy the texture of self-flagellation.

The knots, the tangles, the throat of the thing. I do remember one lover saying "magical" which I took to mean "different." Variable. Lush. Or perhaps just *warm*.

By comparison, I'm surely not that unusual. But I wondered if having not wanted past love could create a physical text that others could read, simply through contact.

Maybe it was my twenties—the desire to feel more than I did when on my back, to be topside more often. But years of sustained disinterest are unrecoverable.

I'm not sure if I agree wholeheartedly with those feminists who argue that half-hearted sex with domestic partners is akin to rape. Carnal acquiescence is a two-way street.

And I'm also not sure about the recent attempt to create a tool for rape prevention based on the concept of the mythical "vagina dentata," or "toothed vagina."

RapeX™ is inserted like a tampon, worn comfortably by a woman, but attaches itself securely to a penis upon penetration. The barbs must be removed by medical personnel.

On the company's website, South African inventor Sonette Ehlers cites a rape victim who inspired her invention by saying, "If only I had teeth down there." *If only*.

South Africa has the highest sexual assault rate of any country on record; I remember this while grappling with the ethics surrounding a thing that many consider "medieval."

In the marriage bed again, it is the wife who has agreed to come back home, to lock the door behind her and be his.

She's tired, the groceries need to be put away. Her head hurts and she's thinking about tomorrow. Still, for him, she may be merely the other Someone there,

for whom consent to marry was *consent given* primary to all others. Maybe I confuse the issue. "Yes" and "no" suffer expirations, of the kind that make provisions.

(Yes today and not tomorrow, or no today and not right now.) Still it hurts him and he sulks. Recall: The separate beds began months into my marriage.

Resignation is easy to understand. When I permitted my ex-husband to move in with me, so he could settle in the city near our son, I felt resigned.

My far-flung boyfriend (Cleveland) and I separated soon after my ex-husband moved in. My privacy and my happiness were gone at once, and my blame had long arms.

Though gone, he overstayed his welcome. These nuances of loss and responsibility do not mean much against what is already over and impossible to recover—my failed romantic dream.

Now I can say "I love you" only to my son without irony. There is no thought to loving anyone else. I have cut my dark hair short.

Still, whenever I go to the dentist, there's some new trouble. Now she says I clench my teeth in my sleep. As a child I ground them incessantly.

But clenching . . . who could know but me? Confessedly, I have opened my eyes with a morning start, teeth like a vise. (What pain is this?)

The terror of losing my teeth to gum recession via bruxism if I don't buy a five-hundred-dollar dental guard almost moves me, but to no avail.

My therapist will profit from my anxieties this time, though they be transmitted through my teeth. Filthy lucre, for each of my masters: Mind, the mouth, my Soul.

Whenever I have looked into dream interpretation regarding teeth, I find them representative of potency or, generally, power. We say colloquially that this or that thing has "teeth."

Absent teeth will never mean anything less than something close for me, like the fear of aging, or my fear of giving up beloved foods, like peanut brittle.

I want to protect myself: against infirmity and acquiescence, or ugliness, infertility, speechlessness. Then there's mortal aversion to decay, the natural dissolution of the body—I fear it.

Or I go because I've never been able or expected to go until now. I've never had a better reason than it's free and only a block away.

(The lady doth protest too much.) Still I rationalize? I craved an essay . . . the self-exposure; *to snap my jaws* to show I still have them.

I bicycled home that afternoon, trying hard to smile without grimacing: numb cheeks, lips, and tongue. People got out of my way. Surely they knew I was dangerous.

Davis McCombs

Tobacco Culture

Then came that moment when they thought again of the river.
Looking up from their work, they thought of fishing there,
of prowling the charred rock shelters on its banks.
They thought of sunlight, still warm and splattering
on the mossy stones, and it pulled them from the fields of stobs,
from the barn's hot tierpoles; it pulled them from the burley,
housed and curing, and they disappeared down cowpaths
at the edge of fields; they slid through stingweed
and the sycamores scabbed with lichen. They carried tackleboxes;
they carried canes; they carried flashlights; the young boy
on the path gripped a flashlight, and its beam was a filament
that reeled him through the gloom of the sloping overhang,
pulling him, step by wobbling step, toward the shelf of stone
above the flood-line and the pipe carved out of banded slate
that was waiting for him there, waiting for centuries in dust
and in the scent of nicotine still clinging to the ash caked in its bowl.

First Hard Freeze

The first hard freeze, an owl beyond the twig
at the window like the shadow of a thought
across the mask of a face, and whatever it is
that will unmask the girl who masks the old
woman who is turning the tap comes crawling

up from timber on a night like this, comes
wandering like wind when everything else
is frosty and still: the deer, unbuckled, the field
a matted bulge, and the flashlight's beam
that will not come to light the fires of their eyes.
On a night like this, the old woman will think
secretly of the dead in their graves, of satin
and of wood and of a dark that pours itself
into a vessel it will never fill. On a night like this,
and in thoughts like these, she is not alone.
The compost hoards its clump of heat; frost
welds the chain to the gate, throwing sparks.
She will lie down to dreams that scatter ahead of her
like snow, but not before she turns the tap one turn,
a hammered metal *drip drip drip* she'll wake to
when a hand not made of hand tests the latch.

q & a

Why does the wolf cock his ear to the wind?
Because the sky at twilight is a mussel shell.

What does he hear?
Note that his guard hairs match the shade between two cedars
perfectly. Note the galaxy mending a net of stars.

What part does the vulture play?
There are sheep beside the fossil bluffs. Steep pastures and a stand of trees.

And the man?
Remember the wind also, ruffling their wool as, in and out of shadow,
the belled flock clanks and bonks and clunks.

Why is he staring toward that dip in the trees?
Imagine the wolf's bass-throated howl of ferocity and darkness and lost
hopes. Or, plot the distance between a buffalo trail and a road paved
with coral.

Why is the road so important?
Because tonight and forever the wolf's howl will remain unanswered.

And what of the girl on the wagon?
She is waiting at the end of many rooms not yet built, down a road
that is still a path through leaves.

How will the story end?
She is dreaming of a book she has been reading about blizzards. She is
thinking that the dead are foxfire.

How long now?
She is considering the distance between lit and burnished.

And is that all?
Between quartz and anthracite?

Will she always be this way?
Look at her there. The trees beside the road are almost grown.

Trash Fish or Nights Back Home

Something must have spooked them.
Something got dumped over the guardrail.
The water under the trestle blurped, convulsed.
It was a good night for a bolt cutter, for hacking something off.
Someone stashed a fruit jar of gizzards in the trunk.

Someone limped across the road in front of the tire repair shop.
It was a good night for tying a guitar string to a treble hook.
A Mustang fish-tailed over gravel, woofers rattling off the bluff.
Someone took a pull off a fifth, passed it.
It was a good night for climbing the water tower,
for jumping the fence. A stigma swam upstream.
Someone pitched a can into the sparks: a good night.
These were the places that demanded, but did not get, a murder.

Karen Salyer McElmurray

That Night

This much is true. My sister was a teller of things to come in that land where we lived then, beside a highway into a town called Smyte. Potholes from coal trucks went by until three AM and not much was alongside us but a country store and the diner, a rattle and slam of car doors in the dark. It's true, the highway is gone now, and the town has become a ghost of itself on the way to bigger towns, and the mountains, too. Lord, looka yonder at them mountaintops, Ruby says, and all she's looking at are the flat-topped tables in the home where she lives. Today she couldn't tell the future anymore even if it was summer, and then again the world was still full of the heat that sent them to us, the men who wanted their fortunes told.

That night, then, Ruby lit incense and draped scarves over the lamps and made ready. Love me in the morning, love me at night. The record she played while she worked went like that. She was a gypsy and a teller of dreams, my sister. She read palms and photographs. She said new-laid eggs buried under a full moon would bring a lover back. Gave out horsetail and stinging nettle, sympathy and just enough hope. Told how love goes around and comes around, Ruby did, even if she could never save anyone. Even herself.

I was fifteen then. Almost as much of a woman as the ones in her magazines, the ladies in high heels with jazz out of open doors at night.

Go on now, girl. She shooed me away with her red silk scarf as she shuffled the poker deck she used to tell fortunes. The cards were old and soft, I knew from all the times I'd laid them out when she wasn't there.

I wanted to be like her, a foreteller of all things.

Can't do a thing with you underfoot. She winked to let me know that when the customers left, she'd pour wine for us both in the leftover jars from jam, a treat I always wanted more than anything else on nights like these.

Most nights I stayed over across the way, at the Black Cat. Sipped a Cherry Coke or sat with Della and Russell and them while they smoked cigarettes on breaks. Ruby liked it there, too. The jukebox and the mopped-up floors, late at night, where her and Russell could cut a shine with Elvis on the jukebox. Russell, him that owned the diner then, and later the company and Smyte and the rest of us that stayed put.

That night I stood for a while and studied the lightning bugs in the mucky field way back. And in front of me that highway I knew like the palm of my own hand. I wanted the cars I saw so bad, the windows rolled down and the soot-tasting air, but all I could do was sit in the metal chair by the mulberry tree and watch my sister. Her shadow floating behind the curtains with the low lights she'd set and that song playing, over and over. Love me, Inez honey, until long past sweet daylight. Shadows put me in mind of the foxes and angels Ruby made for me when I was little, her hands before the blank trailer wall.

From over at the diner the screen door slammed and cars started up by the gas pumps. Voices drifted back. Y'all come on. I'm ready to go. I could have been over there, sitting in a booth and ordering a grilled cheese with pickles on the side. Between orders, Della would talk to me and I'd ask her again. Della. How long have we been around these parts, Ruby and me? Della would tell me stories about her and Russell instead. About nights he'd taken her out dancing the fox trot and how they tasted liquor once that shone with flakes of gold.

Along the highway some truck sliding to a stop in the gravel. Jangly rock 'n' roll and that woman still singing. Inez, honey, hold me in the morning, hold me at night. Boots, maybe. Thudding up our back steps and the trailer door creaking open and slamming shut. Our first customer that night.

Some nights the women came, wanting to see how it felt to sit across a table from a woman with hands as wise as my sister's, her pretty eyes full of love affairs and the foreign places they believed she'd seen. They were afraid of Ruby, and they ought to have been. Her candlelight and her visions, the things she said she knew. The men who came weren't afraid at all. Their faces were hard and they were ready to take what my sister had, whether she knew their futures or not. None of us knew, even me, who she really was or where we came from, my sister and me. We'd lived here all my life, but I didn't know when that began or where.

That night a man's shadow sat at our kitchen table, leaning his big self in toward Ruby. I still imagine his question, easy as honey. You think you can just say that and get by, woman? I imagined her red scarf falling across her shoulders, how she waved it aside. Music rippled the window screen and their shadows bent together. For years I would think of her standing beside the table, her one arm held out. How her hand must have been open, a card in its palm. Maybe, I still tell myself, that card was a good one. Lovers. Two of cups, spilling sweet wine.

And him. Some say it was a man she knew as well as her own self. And some have said it was Russell even, and how she should have known. I ask myself that now, about knowing and remembering, about fortunes and being sure of anything at all. About him or the way the mountains blew apart and how empty the world got then, of coal and love and anything for sure. This much was true. He was a tall man, a taller shadow rounding the table, touching her, both long arms circling her, holding her back. And that music, how it took up what I was seeing. Hold me in the morning, hold me at night. The curtains blew back, fell.

Rain and lightning and behind it thunder and the record still playing. Hold me, hold me. Glass breaking. Voices. Ruby again. You owe me, and that's that. Chair crashing against the floor. I know what I know. A man's voice, so angry it broke open the heavy air. My own name. Waydean. Waydean. My name from Ruby, from inside her mouth and mine. How scared we were.

I'd heard her tell it, how fortune could come that quick, could change you forever. And so it was, a vision of the past and the present that came to while I ran through the yard, up the trailer steps, pushed through a door a million miles from myself. Times tangled up inside me like string for cat's cradle.

I saw the past then. A dirt road, a house, a man who might have been my father walking home for his dinner. Oily potato slices fried in an iron skillet and tossed into a backyard. Come and go light from a kerosene lamp on a table down a hall. The memory of dreams not my own. Muddy waters of a creek on the rise and the pause of someone's feet at a bridge. Wings of hens hanging down as they're carried up a hill. A woman's hands, plucking feathers. Scraps of soap, spoonfuls of lard. A woman bent over a stove, skimming froth off a pot of beans and fatback. Plate by washed plate, leftover signs, crumbs and grease. A room and children and a girl combing her hair and telling stories. Strand by strand, a past I didn't know. The only real vision I'd ever had.

Thunder crashed, took up my vision and the voices and the music from the trailer, took up sounds and crushed it like paper. Hold me, Inez, honey. Hold me all the sweet night long. Thunder become gunshot and then boots crashing down out the back way. A truck door slammed and tires spun gravel and I was holding her, my sister's sweet-salty scent and I pressed my hands against her. It was a wound, that night. It was Ruby and me, and then it was the mountains that took it up, that wound, and soon it was all any of us would know.

Donald Ray Pollock

Real Life

My father showed me how to hurt a man one August night at the Torch Drive-in when I was seven years old. It was the only thing he was ever any good at. This was years ago, back when the outdoor movie experience was still a big deal in southern Ohio. *Godzilla* was playing, along with some sorry-ass flying saucer movie that showed how pie pans could take over the world.

It was hotter than a fat lady's box that evening, and by the time the cartoon began playing on the big plywood screen, the old man was miserable. He kept bitching about the heat, sopping the sweat off his head with a brown paper bag. Ross County hadn't had any rain in two months. Every morning my mother turned the kitchen radio to KB98 and listened to Miss Sally Flowers pray for a thunderstorm. Then she'd go outside and stare at the empty white sky that hung over the holler like a sheet. Sometimes I still think about her standing in that brittle brown grass, stretching her neck in hopes of seeing just one lousy dark cloud.

"Hey, Vernon, watch this," she said that night. Ever since we'd parked, she'd been trying to show the old man that she could stick a hot dog down her throat without messing up her shiny lipstick. You've got to understand, my mother hadn't been out of Knockemstiff all summer. Just seeing a couple of red lights had made her all goosey. But every time she gagged on that wiener, the ropy muscles in the back of my old man's neck twisted a little tighter, made it seem as if his head was going to pop off any second. My older sister, Jeanette, had used her head and played sick all day, then talked them into letting her stay at a neighbor's house. So there I was, stuck in the backseat by myself, chewing the skin off my fingers, and hoping Mom wouldn't piss him off too much before Godzilla stomped the guts out of Tokyo.

But really, it was already too late. Mom had forgotten to pack the old man's special cup, and so everything was shot in the ass as far as he was concerned. He couldn't even muster a chuckle for Popeye, let alone get excited about his wife doing tricks with a wrinkled-up Oscar Mayer. Besides, my old man hated movies. "Screw a bunch of make-believe," he'd say whenever someone mentioned seeing the latest John Wayne or Robert Mitchum. "What the hell's wrong with real life?" He'd only agreed to the drive-in in the first place because of all the hell Mom had raised about his new car, a 1965 Impala he'd brought home the night before.

It was the third set of wheels in a year. We lived on soup beans and fried bread, but drove around Knockemstiff like rich people. Just that morning, I'd heard my mother get on the phone and rage to her sister, the one who lived in town. "The sonofabitch is crazy, Margie," she said. "We couldn't even pay the electric bill last month." I was sitting in front of the dead TV watching watery blood trickle down her pale calves. She'd tried to shave them with the old man's straight razor, but her legs were like sticks of butter. A black fly kept buzzing around her bony ankles, dodging her mad slaps. "I mean it, Margie," she said into the black mouthpiece, "I'd be outta this hellhole in a minute if it wasn't for these kids."

As soon as *Godzilla* started, the old man pulled the ashtray out of the dash and poured a drink in it from his bottle. "Good Lord, Vernon," my mom said. She was holding the hot dog in midair, getting ready to have another go at it.

"Hey, I told you, I ain't drinkin' from no bottle. You start that shit, you end up a goddamn wino." He took a slug from the ashtray, then gagged and spit a soggy cigarette butt out the window. He'd been at it since noon, showing off the new ride to his good-time buddies. There was already a dent in one of the side panels.

After a couple of more sips from the ashtray, the old man jerked the door open and swung his skinny legs out. Puke sprayed from his mouth, soaking the cuffs of his blue work pants with Old Grand-Dad. The station wagon next to us started up and moved to another spot down the row. He hung his head between his legs for a minute or two, then rose up and wiped his chin with the back of his hand. "Bobby," he said to me, "one more your mama's greasy taters and they'll be plantin' your old daddy." My old man didn't eat enough to keep a rat alive, but anytime he threw up his whiskey, he blamed it on Mom's cooking.

Mom gave up, wrapped the hot dog in a napkin, and handed it back to me. "Remember, Vernon," she warned, "you gotta drive us home."

"Shoot," he said, lighting a cigarette, "this car drives its own self." Then he tipped up the ashtray and finished off the rest of his drink. For a few minutes, he stared at the screen and sank slowly into the padded upholstery like a setting sun. My mom reached over and turned the speaker that was hanging in the window down a notch. Our only hope was that the old man would pass out before the entire night was ruined. But as soon as Raymond Burr landed at the Tokyo airport, he shot straight up in his seat, then turned and glared back at me with his bloodshot eyes. "Goddamn it, boy," he said, "how many times I gotta tell you about bitin' them fingernails? You sound like a mouse chewin' through a fuckin' sack of corn."

"Leave him be, Vernon," my mother said. "That ain't what he does anyway."

"Jesus, what's the difference?" he said, scratching the whiskers on his neck. "Hard to tell where he's had those dick skinners."

I pulled my fingers out of my mouth and sat on my hands. It was the only way I could keep away from them whenever the old man was around. That whole summer, he'd been threatening to coat me clear to the elbows with chicken shit to break me of the habit. He splashed more whiskey in his ashtray, and gulped it down with a shudder. Just as I began edging slowly across the seat to sit behind my mother, the dome light popped on. "C'mon, Bobby," he said, "we gotta take a leak."

"But the show just started, Vernon," Mom protested. "He's been waiting all summer to see this."

"Hey, you know how he is," the old man said, loud enough for the people in the next row to hear. "He sees that Godzilla thing, I don't want him pissin' all over my new seats." Sliding out of the car, he leaned against the metal speaker post and stuffed his T-shirt into his baggy pants.

I got out reluctantly and followed my old man as he weaved across the gravel lot. Some teenage girls in culottes strutted by us, their legs illuminated by the movie screen's glimmering light. When he stopped to stare at them, I crashed into the back of his legs and fell down at his feet. "Jesus Christ, boy," he said, jerking me up by the arm like a rag doll, "you gotta get your head out of your ass. You act more like your damn mother every day."

The cinder-block building in the middle of the drive-in lot was swarming with people. The loud rattling projector was up front, the concession stand in the middle, and the johns in the back. The smell of piss and popcorn hung in the hot dead air like insecticide. In the rest-room, a row of men and boys leaned over a long green metal trough with their dicks hanging out. They all stared straight ahead at a wall painted the color of mud. Others were lined up behind them on the wet sticky floor, rocking on the toes of their shoes, impatiently waiting their turn. A fat man in bib overalls and a ragged straw hat tottered out of a wooden stall munching on a Zero candy bar and the old man shoved me inside, slamming the door behind me.

I flushed the commode and stood there holding my breath, pretending to take a leak. Bits and pieces of movie dialogue drifted in from outside and I was trying to imagine the parts I was missing when the old man started banging on the flimsy door. "Damn, boy, what's taking you so long?" he yelled. "You beatin' your meat in there?" He pounded again, and I heard someone laugh. Then he said, "I tell you what, these fuckin' kids will drive you crazy."

I zipped up and stepped out of the stall. The old man was handing a cigarette to a porky guy with sawdust combed through his greasy black hair. A purple stain shaped like a wedge of pie covered the belly of his dirty shirt. "I shit you not, Cappy," my father was telling the man, "this boy's scared of his own goddamn shadow. A fuckin' bug's got more balls."

"Yeah, I know what you mean," Cappy said. He bit the filter off the cigarette and spat it on the concrete floor. "My sister's got one like that. Poor little guy, he can't even bait a hook."

"Bobby shoulda been a girl," the old man said. "Goddamn it, when I was that age, I was choppin' wood for the stove."

Cappy lit the cigarette with a long wooden match he pulled from his shirt pocket and said with a shrug, "Well, things was different back then, Vern." Then he stuck the match in his ear and twirled it around inside his head.

"I know, I know," the old man went on, "but it still makes you wonder what the fuck's gonna happen to this goddamn country someday."

Suddenly a man wearing black-framed glasses stepped from his place in line at the urinal and tapped my old man on the shoulder. He was the biggest sonofabitch I'd ever seen; his fat head nearly touched the ceiling. His arms were the size of fence posts. A boy my size stood behind him, wearing a pair of brightly colored swimming trunks and a T-shirt that had a faded picture of Davy Crockett on the front of it. He had a fresh waxy crew cut and orange pop stains on his chin. Every time he took a breath, a Bazooka bubble bloomed from his mouth like a round pink flower. He looked happy, and I hated him instantly.

"Watch your language," the man said. His loud voice boomed across the room and everyone turned to look at us.

The old man whirled around and rammed his nose into the big man's chest. He bounced back and looked up at the giant towering over him. "Goddamn," he said.

The big man's sweaty face began to turn red. "Didn't you understand me?" he said to my father. "I asked you to watch your cussing. I don't want my son hearing that kind of talk." Then he said slowly, like he was dealing with a retard, "I . . . won't . . . ask . . . you . . . again."

"You didn't ask me the first fuckin' time," my old man shot back. He was tough as bark but rail thin back in those days, and he never knew when to keep his mouth shut. He looked around at the crowd starting to gather, then turned to Cappy and winked.

"Oh, you think it's funny?" the man said. His hands tightened into fists the size of softballs and he made a move toward my father. Someone in the back said, "Kick his ass."

My father took two steps back, dropped his cigarette, and held up his palms. "Now hold on there, buddy. Jesus, I don't mean nothing." Then he lowered his eyes, stood staring at the big man's shiny black shoes for a few seconds. I could see him gnawing on the inside of his mouth. His hands kept opening and closing like the pincers on a crawdad. "Hey," he finally said, "we don't need no trouble here tonight."

The big man glanced at the people watching him. They were all waiting for his next move. His glasses started to slide down his broad nose and he pushed them back up. Taking a deep breath, he swallowed hard, then jabbed a fat finger in my father's bony chest. "Look, I mean what I say," he said, spit flying out his mouth. "This here is a family place. I don't care if you are a damn drunk. You understand?" I sneaked a look over at the man's son and he stuck his tongue out at me.

"Yeah, I understand all right," I heard my father say quietly.

A smug look came over the big bastard's face. His chest puffed out like a tom turkey's, straining the brown buttons on his clean white shirt. Looking around at the pack of men who were hoping to see a fight, he sighed deeply and shrugged his wide shoulders. "I guess that's it, boys," he said to no one in particular. Then, his hand now resting gently on top of his son's head, he started to turn.

I watched nervously as the disappointed crowd shook their heads and began moving away. I remember wishing I could slide out the door with them. I figured the old man would blame me for the way that things had turned out. But just as Godzilla's screechy, door-hinge roar echoed through the restroom, he leaped forward and drove his fist against the temple of the big man's head. People never believe me, but I once saw him knock a horse out with that same hand. A sickening crack reverberated through the concrete room. The man staggered sideways and all of the air suddenly whooshed out his body like a fart. His hands waved frantically in the air as if he were grabbing for a lifeline, and then he dropped to the floor with a thud.

The room went quiet for a second, but when the man's son began screaming, my father exploded. He circled around the man, kicking the ribs with his work boots, stomping the left hand until the gold wedding ring cut through to the bone of his finger. Dropping to his knees, he grabbed the man's glasses and snapped them in two, beat him in the face until a tooth popped through one meaty cheek. Then Cappy and three other men grabbed my father from behind and pulled him away. His fists glistened with blood. A thin string of white froth hung from his chin. I heard someone yell to call the cops. Still holding onto my father, Cappy said, "Jesus, Vern, that man's hurt bad."

Just as I looked up from the body lying on the floor into my father's wild eyes, the man's son turned and drilled me in the ear. I covered up my head with my arms and hunkered down as the boy started to flail away at me. "Goddamn you!" I heard my father yell in a hoarse voice. "You back down, I'll blister your ass!" The hot dogs I'd eaten started to come up, and I swallowed them again. I didn't want to fight, but the boy was nothing compared to the old man. I rose up to face him just as he smacked me in the mouth. I drew back and swung wildly. Somehow I managed to strike him in the face. I heard my father yell again and I kept swinging. After three or four punches, the boy dropped his hands and began blubbering, choking on his bubble gum. I looked over at the old man, and he screamed, "Fuck him up!" I hit the boy again and bright red blood sprayed out his nose.

Breaking loose from the men holding him, my father grabbed me by the arm and pulled me out the doorway. He ran across the parking lot, dragging me along, searching for our car in the dark. Suddenly he stopped and knelt down in front of me. He was gasping for air. "You did good, Bobby," he said, wiping the sweat from his eyes. He gripped me by the shoulders and squeezed. "You did real good."

When we found the car, my father shoved me in the backseat and lifted the speaker off the window. He let it drop to the ground with a bang and jumped in and started the engine. My mother jerked awake. "Is it over?" she asked sleepily. A crackly voice came over the speaker system pleading for any doctors or nurses to report to the concession stand immediately. "Lord, what happened?" Mom said, straightening up in the seat, rubbing her face.

"Some fat sonofabitch tried to tell us how to talk, that's what," the old man said. "But we showed their asses, didn't we, Bobby?" He gunned the motor. We all looked up at the screen just as Godzilla bit into a high-voltage tower. "Holy shit, boy, that thing's got teeth this long," my old man laughed, spreading his arms wide. Then he leaned over and told my mother in a low voice, "They'll call the law on this one." He reached down and dropped the Chevy into gear.

Punching the accelerator, the old man shot off the little mound we were parked on and fishtailed down the aisle. Loose gravel splattered against the other cars. An old man and woman tripped over each other trying to get out of our way. Horns began blowing, headlights popped on. We tore out of the exit and skidded onto the highway, heading west toward home. An ambulance sped by us, its siren blaring. I looked back at the theater just as the movie screen flickered and went black.

"Agnes, you should have seen him," my old man said, pounding the steering wheel with his bloody hand. "He busted the goddamn brat a good one." He grabbed his bottle from under the seat, uncapped it, and took a long slug. "This is the best night of my fucking life!" he yelled out the window.

"You got Bobby in a fight?"

"Damn straight, I did," the old man said.

My mother leaned over the front seat and felt my head with her hands, peered at my face in the dark. "Bobby, are you hurt?" she asked me.

"I got blood on me," I said.

"My God, Vernon," she said. "What have you done now, you sick bastard?"

I looked up as he bashed my mother with his forearm. Her head bounced against the window. "You sonofabitch!" she cried, covering her face with her hands.

"Don't baby him," the old man said. "And don't call me no bastard neither."

I scooted across the seat and sat behind my father as we raced home. Every time he passed a car, he took another pull from the bottle. Wind rushed through his open window and dried my sweat. The Impala felt like it was floating above the highway. *You did good*, I kept saying to myself, over and over. It was the only goddamn thing my old man ever said to me that I didn't try to forget.

Later the sound of an approaching storm woke me up. I was lying in my bed, still in my clothes. Through my window, I saw lightning flash over the Mitchell Flats. A rumbling wall of thunder rolled across the holler, followed closely by a high, horrible wail, and I thought of Godzilla and the movie that I'd missed. It was only after the thunder faded into the distance that I realized that the wail was just the sound of my old man getting sick in the bathroom.

My bedroom door opened and my mother walked in holding a lighted candle. "Bobby?" she said. I pretended to be asleep. She leaned over me, brushed my sore cheek with her soft hand. Then she reached up and closed my window. In the candlelight, I sneaked a look at the bruise spreading across her face like a smear of grape jelly.

She tiptoed out of the room, leaving the door ajar, and walked down the hall. "There," I heard her say to my father, "is that better?"

"I think I fucked it up," my father said. "That bastard's head was hard as a rock."

"You shouldn't drink, Vernon," my mom said.

"Is he asleep?"

"He's wore out."

"I'd bet a paycheck he broke that kid's nose, the way the blood came out," my father said.

"We better go to bed," my mom said.

"I couldn't believe it, Agnes. That fucking kid was twice Bobby's size, I swear to God."

"He's just a boy, Vernon."

They walked slowly past my door, leaning into each other, and went into their bedroom. I heard my mother say, "No way," but then after a few minutes, their bed began to squeak like a rusty seesaw. Outside, the storm finally cut loose, and big drops of rain began pounding the tin roof of the house. I heard my mother moan, my father call out for Jesus. A bolt of lightning arced across the black sky, and long shadows moved about on the bare plaster walls of my room. I pulled the thin sheet over my head and stuck my fingers in my mouth. A sweet, salty taste stung my busted lip, ran over my tongue. It was the other boy's blood, still on my hands.

As my parents' bed thumped loudly against the floor in the next room, I lapped the blood off my knuckles. The dried flakes dissolved in my mouth, turning my spit to syrup. Even after I'd swallowed all the blood, I kept licking my hands. I tore at the skin with my teeth. I wanted more. I would always want more.

Sara Pritchard

The Very Beautiful Sad Elegy for Bambi's Dead Mother

1952—You are two years old and eating a book. Albertine is four and reading aloud *James James Morrison Morrison Weatherby George.* . . . You wish that she'd shut up. The spine of your book is gold and particularly tasty. You gnaw on it with your front teeth like it's an ear of corn. *Baby's House* the book says on its chipboard cover. *This is baby's house* . . . the Little Golden Book begins, the text running underneath a bright illustration of a white clapboard house with a green roof.

This is baby's living room . . . the next page continues, on and on—a real page-turner—through the traditional American home of the Truman and Eisenhower years: baby's dining room, baby's kitchen, up the stairs to baby's parents' room (twin beds), baby's brother's room, baby's bedroom . . . but your favorite room is baby's bathroom. In baby's bathroom, baby stands on a bright red bench beside a big clawfoot bathtub and brushes her teeth in front of a medicine cabinet mirror.

This is *your* bathroom, too. You also have a big clawfoot bathtub—big enough for your mother, your sister Albertine, and you to fit in all together—and a bench painted bright red, a brown door with a ceramic doorknob and a shiny silver lock that goes *click-click click-click*—like your brother Mason's pocket cricket—when you turn it back and forth, back and forth, back and forth, back and forth. . . .

1955—The bathroom of the house at 41 Cherry Street in Ashport, Pennsylvania, has great acoustics: a high ceiling with a light you turn on and off by pulling a long string with a crocheted tassel, and a checker-board floor of black and white tiles. There's a tiny window with frosted glass that pushes out and affords an excellent, bird's-eye view of the alley, Go-Jeff's dog house, the cherry tree decorated with its white caterpillar tents, and the clothesline with its chorus line of laundry. There's a radiator, too, for help climbing from the stool onto the sink, and above the sink a medicine cabinet with a mirror and chock-full of salves, Band-Aids, various cold and stomach-upset remedies, plus iodine and mercurochrome in tiny brown bottles with glass sticks. There is also a tall metal locker painted white, which smells inside of Cashmere Bouquet and with two shelves of scratchy towels, *plus*—to your five-year-old wonder—magnificent and curious things in the bottom like a toilet plunger, which is really a combination pogo stick, wall sucker, and marching hat; a box of some kind of mattresses for the beds in a mouse hospital; a black rubber pear with a hole in one end and a little snoot, which is for puffing dead flies off the windowsill; a big vitamin-colored rubber bag with a long, black rubber straw, which can glug up toilet water and other things; and—on the door—A LOCK!

Locked in the bathroom at 41 Cherry Street after morning half-day kindergarten, while your father is out working for Atlas Powder Company, your sister Albertine and your brother Mason at school, and your mother doing laundry or teaching piano lessons downstairs, you spend many happy hours laying out crayons on the radiator and watching them melt, tap dancing on the tile floor while singing the McGuire Sisters' "Sugartime" or Burl Ives's "Big Rock Candy Mountain," playing Albertine's flutophone (which she keeps hidden in a Buster Brown shoebox under the bed and which you are forbidden to touch), eating Vicks VapoRub out of the jar with your finger, sipping Cheracol cough syrup, watching St. Joseph's aspirin for children dissolve on your tongue, taking your clothes off and examining every square inch of your body with your mother's hand mirror, shaving the hair off your arms with your father's Gillette razor, or standing on the bright red bench, staring into the medicine cabinet mirror on the opposite wall and repeating endlessly your favorite phrase in many different voices, pronunciations, variations, accents, and volumes:

Yellow Velvet.
YEL-LOH VEL-VET!

yel-LOW vel-VET.

YEL-low VEL-velt.

YEL-low vel-VET

VELVET YELLOW

VELLOW YELVET

VellowyYellowysmellowyVELVET

yellowvelvetyellowvelvetyellowvelvet.

YALLLLLOUH VALL-VETTTT!

Now you are a little older and learning to read and write. There are many wonderful words to say and write and spell, but the most glorious, wonderful word of all is SQUIRREL. SQUIRREL with its big, swirling S, its magnificent Q with the long squirrelly tail, its dog-barking R-R. SQUIRREL is a word to be written in the dirt in the alley with a stick, to be written with your finger on the side of your father's DeSoto and on steamed-up windows in the kitchen and in the coffee-table dust and on the television screen. With one of your father's mechanical pencils, SQUIRREL can be written very small on the wallpaper going up the stairs or low to the floor, just above the molding, or longways, marching up the corner of Mason's room.

In blue ballpoint ink, SQUIRREL can be printed in Mason's trigonometry book, on your Aunt Frannie Linn's playing cards, on dollar bills in your mother's wallet, and inside Albertine's Buster Brown shoes. With the mechanical pencil point, the word SQUIRREL can be scratched into the back of wooden doors and on bureaus underneath doilies, and on the headboard of your bed. One night in bed you think of SQUIRREL backwards, and the magical word LERRIUQS, pronounced Larry Ukus (the Mighty Mouse of squirrels) appears in blue ink on your sheets. Brushing your teeth one morning and looking in the mirror, an even *more* magical word appears on one of the white horizontal stripes on your pajama top where the word squirrel had once been printed.

Life is beautiful.

But briefly. You are no longer allowed to have a pencil, a pen, a crayon, a piece of chalk, nor any other writing instrument on your person without supervision. For an hour—Dale Evans time—you must sit quietly in your room and think about what you have done, and it is during this very thoughtful, quiet period that Blinker comes up with the idea of invisible writing: writing with water. Blinker is the person who fed Betsy Wetsy a bottle of real milk and then put her to bed without making her pee, and a rank odor began to spread from your corner of the bedroom. Blinker is the person who drank the entire bottle of Cheracol and then threw up in the hall. It's a damn good thing he threw up, too, or he could be dead or in St. Vincent's getting his stomach pumped. Blinker is the person whose breath smells like Vicks VapoRub. Blinker is the person responsible for the cricket lock on the bathroom door now rusting in a Chase & Sanborn can in the basement.

After this quiet, thoughtful hour is up, Blinker must go to the bathroom. There, Blinker experiments on a very small scale with the first invisible water writing, and it is quite successful, but Blinker cannot leave well enough alone. During dinner that evening, eating corn on the cob, Blinker comes up with the concept of butter writing. Butter writing is a kind of shiny water writing. After dinner, with a purloined stick of Land O'Lakes, Blinker writes the word SQUIRREL on the wallpaper behind the davenport and then gives the remainder of the stick of butter to Go-Jeff, who gulps it down whole, paper and all. The next day while your mother is doing laundry, butter writing progresses to Crisco writing and escalates to Crisco erasing, which involves big globs of Crisco necessary to erase or blend together shiny spots on the wallpaper, leaving the can of Crisco full of dust and dog hair and big patches of the wallpaper a dark pee-colored yellow.

Blinker has really done it this time. You fear for your life, so you go upstairs and get in your bed and pull the covers up over your head. Downstairs, your mother comes in the back door with a laundry basket. She walks into the living room and sets the basket on the davenport.

"What's this?" she says, but you cannot hear her because you are taking a nap, you are sound asleep. Because you're sick. Because you have a terrible stomachache. Because you're dying. You are sound asleep and dying at the same time. You're snoring loudly, as only dying people with stomachaches can snore: *Ckckcooonkckck. Ckckcooooooonkckck.*

Your mother is coming up the stairs calling your name. "Ruby!" she calls, "Ruby Jean Reese!"

Should you add the whistling exhale like in the Bugs Bunny cartoons or would that be too much?

Ckcknnkckck. Pffffwwwwwww. Ckckcnnnkckck. Pffffwwwwwww.

a few days later

You're sitting on the davenport with your bride doll on your lap, your brother Mason beside you. You're watching *Mighty Mouse,* and Mason says to you, without turning his head:

"So did you hear about that buddy of yours, that er—Blinker, is it?—fella, Blinker the famous Crisco painter?"

"What about Blinker?" you ask.

"He bought the ranch," Mason says.

"What ranch?"

"He turned up dead, stupid."

"Did not."

"Did."

"Did not."

"It was on the radio . . . last night . . . while you were asleep. Blinker was run over by a truck and decapitated."

"Well, maybe he got run over by a truck and he was declumpertated, but he's OK," you insist. (Blinker had been run over by a truck on one other occasion, but it turned out to have been a mistake. It was somebody else.)

"He got his stomach pumped and now he's OK," you elaborate. "Dr. Elsworth said he's OK."

"Yeah, he's OK alright. He's just fine without a head!" Your brother Mason starts laughing hysterically and beating on one of the davenport's fat arms. "Yeah," he laughs, "he's just gotta big canna Crisco where his head used to be! Ha-ha! Ha-ha! Ha-ha-ha-ha-ha! Ha-ha! Ha-ha! Ha-ha-ha-ha-ha!"

"Whadda mean, without a head? Blinker's got a head. He does too got a head!"

"No, stupid, he's been DE-CAP-I-TATED. You don't even know what DE-CAP-I-TATED means. It's too big a word for you."

"Shut up. I do, too, know what D-coppertated means."

"D-coppertated!!! Ha-ha-ha! Ha-ha-he-he-ha-ha! You can't even pronounce it! Ha-Ha-ha! Ha-ha-ha! Ha-ha-he-he! So what does D-coppertated mean, Smartypants?"

Silence.

"DE-CAP-I-TATED means he got his head got cut off!" Mason says. "Blinker got his head cut off. Just picture Blinker's head rolling down the street like a basketball. Ha-ha-ha-ha! Ho-ho-ho-ho! He-he-he-he-he!"

"Don't tell her a thing like that!" your mother scolds. She is passing by the living room and has overheard Mason's remark. She walks around the corner and swats your brother on the back of his head with a tea towel and then leaves.

You watch some more *Mighty Mouse*, and then it's over. *Sky King* comes on, then *Sergeant Preston of the Yukon*.

"How do you spell that clumpertated word?" you turn and ask Mason.

"I believe in the holey ghost, the holey Christian church, the communion of saints, the forgiveness of sins, the resurrection of the body, and the life everlasting, hey men!" you say to yourself, bouncing a ball, walking Go-Jeff on a make-believe leash, jumping rope, hopping on one foot, skipping to school, whumping your Slinky down the stairs. "The life everlasting, hey men! The life everlasting, *hey men!* The holey Christian church. The holey Christian church. The holey-moley, roly-poly, holey Christian church."

Now it's Thanksgiving vespers, and after your favorite poem, the Apostles' Creed, everyone is singing one of your favorite hymns, "Bringing in the Cheese," their voices happy and cheerful, their faces kind in the yellow light. Mrs. Kline, at the pipe organ, is trying to keep up, her crow wings flapping, her feet going one direction, her hands the other.

> *Bringing in the cheese, bringing in the cheese,*
> *We shall come rejoicing, bringing in the cheese.*

You stand next to Albertine in the children's choir and sing as loud as you can, sort of shouting. You sing with your top lip curled under and your top teeth sticking out like a mouse because this is a hymn written by church mice, and you are pretending to be one of them as you sing. Gus and Jacques—from *Cinderella*—probably had a part in composing this wonderful hymn. They probably know it by heart. They are probably singing it right now at the top of their lungs in one of the dark, echoing alcoves of Riverview Lutheran Church, maybe over to your right, there behind the baptismal pot, standing on a big hunk of Swiss cheese.

The hymn is over. The congregation claps shut their hymnals, but everyone remains standing as Mason, an acolyte, puts out the altar candles with the big candlesnuffer on a pole. Reverend Creech raises his arms like he, too, is about to fly. "Let us pray," he says, and then the beautiful words wash over you, the words you will always remember all the long days of your life and whisper to yourself when you are afraid, when you are alone, when all the sadness of being human gathers itself around you:

> *May the piece of God, which passeth all understanding,*
> *keep your hearts and minds in Christ Jesus, Amen.*

For many, many years you ponder just exactly which piece of God Reverend Creech might be referring to, but for now, you forget about all that because the choir is filing out and everyone is singing your very most favorite song in the whole world, the one your mother plays for you on the piano at bedtime, and your father has taught you and Albertine to sing in two-part harmony:

> *Now the day is over, night is drawing nigh,*
> *Shadows of the evening steal across the sky.*
> *Now the darkness gathers, stars begin to peep,*
> *Birds and beasts and flowers soon will be asleep.*
> *Thru the long night watches may thine angels spread*
> *Their white wings above me watching 'round my bed.*

Grant to little children visions bright of Thee;
Guard the sailors tossing on the deep blue sea.
Comfort every sufferer watching late in pain;
Those who plan some evil, from their sin restrain.
Jesus, give the weary calm and sweet repose;
With Thy tenderest blessing may mine eyelids close.

1958—With very little coaxing and carrying, and only minor scratches, a big orange cat follows you and Albertine home from school. A big orange cat with silky fur and a big round pumpkin head. An orange cat who walks around the house rubbing her head on the legs of everything, including you. She walks in and out your legs, in and out, and her tail goes up your dress and makes you giggle.

"Our cat must have a very beautiful name," Albertine announces. "Princess!" she exclaims. "Here, Princess! Here pretty Princess Kitty!"

"Kyrie Eleison!" you call, after the beautiful and mysterious words of the Kyrie sung in church. "Here, Kyrie," you call, crawling across the carpet toward your cat. "Here Kyrie! Kyrie Eleison!"

"Daisy," Albertine says resolutely. "DAISY BUTTERCUP."

"Here Dona, Here Dona," you persist, "Here Dona Nobis Pacem!" and Albertine rolls her eyes so far back into her head they disappear completely. Only the whites—like Orphan Annie's—show.

"Panis Angelicus?" you pout and beg, "Adeste Fideles? Agnus Dei?"

For many hours that night, you lie awake, wandering through the enchanted forest of all the words you know, bumping into trunks and branches, tripping over roots and stumps, searching for the perfect name for your beautiful orange cat: mimosa, marmalade, gladiola, peony, poppycock, forsythia, taffeta, pinochle, piano forte, aspen, pumpkinseed, Leviticus Numbers, lickety-split, fiddlesticks, Worcestershire, nincompoop, whippoorwill, whippersnapper, Frigidaire, DeSoto, squirrel, pollywollydoodle all the day . . . and on and on. And then . . . lying on its back, humming "Row, Row, Row Your Boat," kicking its feet and doing the backstroke around your brain, you find it: the perfect name for your cat. So you can go to sleep now. But come morning, you wake up in a panic because the perfect name has now escaped you! You should have written it down! Your heart is racing: mimosa, gladiola, peony, for-sythia, taffeta, squirrel . . . Oh, praise the Lord, there it is! You run downstairs, but . . .

Your cat is gone.

"He wanted out," Mason mumbles, dripping a big, sloppy serving-spoonful of Wheaties up to his mouth and never looking up from the cereal box he is reading.

Other than the time Mr. Rossi crawled out on his roof and hollered for everyone to turn themselves into little children and the time Mrs. Wagner's pressure cooker exploded split pea soup, there is not much excitement in Ashport. Except on Saturday. Every Saturday, you and Albertine walk to the Strand Theater on Broad Street. Matinees start at noon with double features that last until four o'clock. Every single kid in Ashport is there, it seems. Ushers dressed like Johnny Philip Morris unhook the velvet sausages and you pour in like lava, hundreds of you racing down the aisles and up the steps to the balconies, you and Albertine running, too, holding hands. The ushers close the doors and slouch around the lobby, smoking Old Golds, reading magazines, and playing cards, betting pennies, never paying you any mind until they open the doors hours later. Until then, behind the closed doors, it's may-hem, a zoo. The Strand has two balconies; a gilded, domed ceiling; and tiered side-boxes like the ones in Ford's Theatre where Lincoln was shot—two- and four-seaters with heavy maroon curtains. Kids are everywhere, screaming, running, hanging off the balconies like apes, choking on popcorn, losing their fillings and swallowing their teeth along with Jujubes, throwing wads of Bazooka bubble gum at the screen, and making elephant noises with empty Good & Plenty boxes.

You'll watch *A Light in the Forest* and *Johnny Tremain*; *Westward Ho, the Wagons!*; *20,000 Leagues Under the Sea*; and *Tarzan the Ape Man*, and there at the Strand you'll see *Old Yeller*. There will not be a peep out of anyone when Travis discovers Old Yeller has rabies. Everyone knows what Travis must do. All the children at the Strand will be sniffling, boo-hooing, wiping their snotty noses on their sleeves as Travis raises his twenty-two.

Shortly after *Old Yeller*, Walt Disney's *Bambi* will come to the Strand, and around the same time, your father will begin reading you and Albertine *The Yearling*. Next, he will read you a cherished book from his own childhood about an orphaned grizzly bear cub named Wahb. Quickly and wholeheartedly you will begin to embrace the morose romanticism of female pubescence, priming yourself for the death of Beth in *Little Women,* a passage which Albertine reads to you every night in bed.

The Saturday you see *Bambi*, though, you will begin your life's work as a writer and editor, an epic poem entitled "The Very Beautiful Sad Elegy for Bambi's Dead Mother." That is your poem's final title, but it will go through literally hundreds of titles and revisions as you work on it over the next three years. "The Very Beautiful Sad Elegy for Bambi's Dead Mother" isn't just any old elegy. It is a very special genre: an illustrated elegy. Crying fawns standing on their hind legs and wiping their eyes with floral handkerchiefs crowd the side margins. Stiff dead deer with their legs sticking up in the air like upside-down coffee tables adorn the bottom. And, throughout, there is a lot of corn—corn on the cob and the Jolly Green Giant canned variety, too—because you know deer like corn, and for some reason you feel the poem should have both visual and taste appeal for deer. Today, your "Very Beautiful Sad Elegy for Bambi's Dead Mother" could pass as a long-lost collaborative effort between Rod McKuen, Andy Warhol, and Betty Crocker.

Here's the first stanza of the final version of your poem, "The Very Beautiful Sad Elegy for Bambi's Dead Mother":

> *In the meadow still and calm,*
> *Lays the lovely stag.*
> *Never will she run again,*
> *Nor never leap the crag.*

You know the word *elegy* because it is the name of a song you learned to play on your Grandpa Doc's trombone. At first you played it as fast as possible, like you play everything else, but when your mother told you to slow down, it was supposed to be sad because somebody died, everything seemed to miraculously come together—music, art, movies, fairy tales, poetry—like the missing piece of a jigsaw puzzle showing up at the bottom of a shoebox full of broken crayons.

You decide on the synonym *stag* for deer after casually asking everyone you know: "Excuse me, excuse me, excuse me, what's another word for 'deer'?" Your brother Mason offers you *stag,* a wonderful word, a great gift. Likewise, *crag* would be found by asking people the meaning of every possible word you can come up with that rhymes with *stag,* as in, "Excuse me, is 'klag' a word?"

In fact, the whole poem will be written pretty much that way. You have never heard of a thesaurus, although you are learning to use your father's *Webster's* dictionary.

You repeat this poem to yourself all the time and work on it every day after school in a very ritualistic fashion. You keep it rolled up, with a rubber band around it, in a black metal miner's lunch pail that your father has given you, along with some broken crayons, a mechanical pencil your brother Mason has been looking for for some time, a beautiful fountain pen on loan from your mother, a jar of Sheaffer's blue ink, a candle stub, and some books of matches from the Knotty Pine. The fountain pen is a dark, marbled blue, with a little metal lever on the side that lets the pen suck up ink like an elephant's trunk. The poem is written on very thin graph paper (also from your father) with a pale blue grid.

You keep the lunch pail under your bed. Every day after school, you crawl under the bed, retrieve the lunch pail, and take it up into the attic where you light the candle and work on your chef-d'oeuvre. It is all very difficult—the writing and drawing on the uneven, splintery floor boards, the curling paper, the fountain pen and all, but this is the path you've chosen.

The only person you ever show your poem to is your mother, to whom you read it many, many times, every revision. Every time you sit on your mother's lap and read her "The Very Beautiful Sad Elegy for Bambi's Dead Mother," she hugs you and then puts her hand over her heart and says, "Sweetheart, that's really, really beautiful. I know you will be a famous poet someday, Ruby Jean."

When you are nine, though, in September 1959, you start fourth grade with a young, pretty teacher, Miss Barrett. Miss Barrett is just out of state teachers' college. She is very stylish, with short fawn-colored hair. Miss Barrett wears muted cashmere twin-set sweaters and a single strand of pearls with a big gold clip. You have always been quite shy, but you trust Miss Barrett with her fawn-colored hair and fawn-colored camel's hair coat, her fawn-colored sweaters and white pearls, and you really want her to like you. After much deliberation, one fall Friday when school is over and Miss Barrett is in the front of the room erasing the blackboards, you tiptoe up to her desk and place "The Very Beautiful Sad Elegy for Bambi's Dead Mother" on it, rolled up and tied with a hair ribbon, and tiptoe away. All weekend you daydream about Miss Barrett reading your poem, imagining that she will love your poem, love you, praise you. She will probably come to school on Monday, you speculate, with her eyes all red and puffy from crying.

On Monday morning, you put on your favorite dress—black watch plaid with a big white Pilgrim collar and a black velvet bow—and your patent-leather Mary Janes. Miss Barrett is wearing her tan cashmere sweater, her white pearls, and her camel's hair skirt—her most fawn-like ensemble. She is walking up and down the aisles, calling names, taking roll, something in her hand with a rib— . . . *Could it.* . . .

When she calls your name, Miss Barrett places "The Very Beautiful Sad Elegy for Bambi's Dead Mother" on your desk—without a word—in front of the whole class—and pats you on the head. Embarrassed, you stuff the rolled-up poem quickly into your plaid bookbag.

All day you feel sick.

After school, you run home, Go-Jeff nipping at your heels, and race upstairs to the attic stairwell, throw open the door, heart pounding, and click it shut. Unbuckle your bag and unroll "The Very Beautiful Sad Elegy for Bambi's Dead Mother."

On the first page, in Miss Barrett's big, neat hand, is printed in red ink: *A stag is a* male *deer!!!* Three exclamation marks and a thick red underline like a bad cut.

A little ways down the page and running right over a particularly poignant fawn (possibly even Bambi herself), a thick red circle is drawn around the word *lay,* and in the margin Miss Barrett has written the words: *Only chickens lay!!!* Three more big red exclamation marks like war paint and, again, the thick red underscore like an open wound.

You are overcome with shame and humiliation and tears. Into your room you run, banging the door, and under the bed you crawl and grab the black miner's pail. Up the attic stairs you fly with your pail and your stupid elegy poem, your Mary Janes flashing, and into the attic closet, where you kick the door again and again and strike the matches and set that stupid poem that goddamn stupid holey shit Christian goddamn beautiful sad piss-on-it damn elegy on fire.

Ron Rash

Back of Beyond

When Parson drove to his shop that morning, the sky was the color of lead. Flurries settled on the pickup's windshield, lingered a moment before expiring. A heavy snow tonight, the weatherman warned, and it looked to be certain, everything getting quiet and still, waiting. Even more snow in the higher mountains, enough to make many roads impassable. It would be a profitable day, because Parson knew they'd come to his pawnshop to barter before emptying every cold-remedy shelf in town. They would hit Wal-Mart first because it was cheapest, then the Rexall, and finally the town's three convenience stores, coming from every way-back cove and hollow in the county, because walls and windows couldn't conceal the smell of meth.

Parson pulled his jeep into the parking lot of the cinder-block building with PARSON'S BUY AND SELL hung over the door. One of the addicts had brought an electric portable sign last week, had it in his truck bed with a trash can filled with red plastic letters to stick on it. The man told Parson the sign would ensure that potential customers noticed the pawnshop. You found me easy enough, Parson had replied. His watch said eight forty and the sign in the window said nine to six Tuesday through Saturday, but a gray decade-old Ford Escort had already nosed up to the building. The back windshield was damaged, cracks spreading outward like a spiderweb. The gas cap a stuffed rag. A woman sat in the driver's seat. She could have been waiting ten minutes or ten hours.

Parson got out of his truck, unlocked the door, and cut off the alarm. He turned on the lights and walked around the counter, placed the loaded Smith & Wesson revolver on the shelf below the register. The copper bell above the sill tinkled.

The woman waited in the doorway, a wooden butter churn and dasher clutched in her arms. Parson had to hand it to them, they were getting more imaginative. Last week the electric sign and false teeth, the week before that four bicycle tires and a chiropractic table. Parson nodded for the woman to come on in. She set the churn and dasher on the table.

"It's a antique," the woman said. "I seen one like it on TV and the fellow said it was worth a hundred dollars."

When the woman spoke, Parson glimpsed the stubbed brown ruin inside her mouth. He could see her face clearly now, sunken cheeks and eyes, skin pale and furrowed. He saw where the bones, impatient, poked at her cheeks and chin. The eyes glossy but alive, restless and needful.

"You better find that fellow then," Parson said. "A fool like that don't come around often."

"It was my great-grandma's," the woman said, nodding at the churn, "so it's near seventy-five years old." She paused. "I guess I could take fifty for it."

Parson looked the churn over, lifted the dasher and inspected it as well. An antiques dealer in Asheville might give him a hundred.

"Twenty dollars," Parson said.

"That man on TV said . . ."

"You told me," Parson interrupted. "Twenty dollars is what I'll pay."

The woman looked at the churn a few moments, then back at Parson.

"Okay," she said.

She took the cash and stuffed the bills in her jeans. She did not leave.

"What?" Parson asked.

The woman hesitated, then raised her hands and took off her high school ring. She handed it to him, and Parson inspected it. "Class of 2000," the ring said.

"Ten," he said, laying the ring on her side of the glass counter.

She didn't try to barter this time but instead slid the ring across the glass as if it were a piece in a board game. She held her fingers on the metal a few moments before letting go and holding out her palm.

By noon he'd had twenty customers and almost all were meth addicts. Parson didn't need to look at them to know. The odor of it came in the door with them, in their hair, their clothes, a sour ammonia smell like cat piss. Snow fell steady now and his business began slacking off, even the manic needs of the addicted deferring to the weather. Parson was finishing his lunch in the back room when the bell sounded again. He came out and found Sheriff Hawkins waiting at the counter.

"So what they stole now, Doug?" Parson asked.

"Couldn't it be I just come by to see my old high school buddy?"

Parson placed his hands on the counter.

"It could be, but I got the feeling it isn't."

"No," Hawkins said, smiling wryly. "In these troubled times there's not much chance to visit with friends and kin."

"Troubled times," Parson said. "But good for business, not just my business but yours."

"I guess that's a way of looking at it, though for me it's been too good of late."

Hawkins took a quick inventory of the bicycles and lawn mowers and chain saws filling the room's corners. Then he looked the room over again, more purposeful this time, checking behind the counter as well. The sheriff's brown eyes settled on the floor, where a shotgun lay amid other items yet to be tagged.

"That .410 may be what I'm looking for," the sheriff said. "Who brought it in?"

"Danny."

Parson handed the gun to the lawman without saying anything else. Hawkins held the shotgun and studied the stock a moment.

"My eyes ain't what they used to be, Parson, but I'd say them initials carved in it are SJ, not DP."

"That gun Steve Jackson's?"

"Yes, sir," the sheriff replied, laying the shotgun on the counter. "Danny took it out of Steve's truck yesterday. At least that's what Steve believed."

"I didn't notice the initials," Parson said. "I figured it came off the farm."

Hawkins picked the shotgun off the counter and held it in one hand, studying it critically. He shifted it slightly, let his thumb rub the stock's varnished wood.

"I think I can talk Steve out of pressing charges."

"Don't do that as a favor to me," Parson said. "If his own daddy don't give a damn he's a thief, why should I?"

"How come you to think Ray doesn't care?" Hawkins asked.

"Because Danny's been bringing things to me from the farm for months. Ray knows where they're going. I called him three months ago and told him myself. He said he couldn't do anything about it."

"Doesn't look to be you're doing much about it either," the sheriff said. "I mean, you're buying from him, right?"

"If I don't he'll just drive down to Sylva and sell it there."

Parson looked out at the snow, the parking lot empty but for his and Hawkins's vehicles. He wondered if any customers had decided not to pull in because of the sheriff's car.

"You just as well go ahead and arrest him," Parson added. "You've seen enough of these meth addicts to know he'll steal something else soon enough."

"I didn't know he was on meth," Hawkins said.

"That's your job, isn't it," Parson replied, "to know such things?"

"There's too many of them to keep up with. This meth, it ain't like other drugs. Even cocaine and crack, at least those were expensive and hard to get. But this stuff, it's too easy." The sheriff looked out the window. "This snow's going to make for a long day, so I'd better get to it."

"So you're not going to arrest him?"

"No," Hawkins said. "He'll have to wait his turn. There's two dozen in line ahead of him. But you could do me a favor by giving him a call. Tell him this is his one chance, that next time I'll lock his ass up." Hawkins pressed his lips together a moment, pensive. "Hell, he might even believe it."

"I'll tell him," Parson said, "but I'll do it in person."

Parson went to the window and watched as the sheriff backed out onto the two-lane and drove toward the town's main drag. Snow stuck to the asphalt now, the jeep blanketed white. He'd watched Danny drive away the day before, the tailgate down and truck bed empty. Parson had known the truck bed would probably be empty when Danny headed out of town, no filled grocery bags or kerosene cans, because the boy lived in a world where food and warmth and clothing were no longer important. The only essentials were the red-and-white packs of Sudafed in the passenger's seat as the truck disappeared back into the folds of the higher mountains, headed up into Chestnut Cove, what Parson's father had called the back of beyond, the place where Parson and Ray had grown up.

He placed the pistol in his coat pocket and changed the OPEN sign to CLOSED. Once on the road, Parson saw the snow was dry, powdery, which would make the drive easier. He headed west and did not turn on the radio.

Except for two years in the army, Ray had lived his whole life in Chestnut Cove. He'd used his army pay to buy a farm adjacent to the one he'd grown up on and had soon after married Martha. Parson had joined the army as well but afterward went to Tuckasegee to live. When their parents had gotten too old to mend fences and feed livestock, plant and harvest the tobacco, Ray and Martha did it. Ray had never asked Parson to help, never expected him to, since he was twenty miles away in town. For his part, Parson had not been bitter when the farm was willed to the firstborn. Ray and Martha had earned it. By then Parson owned the pawnshop outright from the bank, had money enough. Ray and Martha sold their house and moved into the farmhouse, raised Danny and his three older sisters there.

Parson slowed as the road began a long curve around Brushy Mountain. The road soon forked and he went left. Another left and he was on a county road, poorly maintained because no wealthy Floridians had second homes on it. No guardrails. He met no other vehicle, because only a few people lived in the cove, had ever lived up here.

Parson parked beside Ray's truck and got out, stood a few moments before the homestead. He hadn't been up in nearly a year and supposed he should feel more than the burn of anger directed at his nephew. Some kind of nostalgia. But Parson couldn't summon it, and if he had, then what for? Working his ass off in August tobacco fields, milking cows on mornings so cold his hands numbed—the very things that had driven him away in the first place. Except for a thin ribbon of smoke unfurling from the chimney, the farm appeared forsaken. No cattle huddled against the snow, no TV or radio playing in the front room or kitchen. Parson had never regretted leaving, and never more so than now as his gaze moved from the rusting tractor and bailer to the sagging fences that held nothing in, settled on the shambling farmhouse itself, then turned toward the land between the barn and house.

Danny's battered blue-and-white trailer squatted in the pasture. Parson's feet made a whispery sound as he went to deal with his nephew before talking to his brother and sister-in-law. No footprints marked the snow between house and trailer. Parson knocked on the flimsy aluminum door and when no one answered went in. No lights were on and Parson wasn't surprised when he flipped a switch and nothing happened. His eyes slowly adjusted to the room's darkness, and he saw the card table, on it cereal boxes, some open, some not, a half-gallon milk container, its contents frozen solid. The room's busted-out window helped explain why. Two bowls scabbed with dried cereal lay on the table as well. Two spoons. Parson made his way to the back room, seeing first the kerosene heater beside the bed, the wire wick's muted orange glow. Two closely lumped mounds rose under a pile of quilts. *Like they're already laid out in their graves*, Parson thought as he leaned over and poked the bigger form.

"Get up, boy," Parson said.

But it was Ray's face and torso that emerged, swaddled in an array of shirts and sweaters. Martha's face appeared as well. They seemed like timid animals disturbed in their dens. For a few moments Parson could only stare at them. After decades in the most cynical of professions, he was amazed that anything could still stun him.

"Why in the hell aren't you in the house?" Parson asked finally.

It was Martha who replied.

"Danny, he's in there, sometimes his friends too." She paused. "It's just better, easier, if we're out here."

Parson looked at his brother. Ray was sixty-five years old but he looked eighty, his mouth sunk in, skinny and feeble. His sister-in-law appeared a little better off, perhaps because she was a large, big-boned woman. But they both looked bad—hungry, weary, sickly. And scared. Parson couldn't remember his brother ever being scared, but he clearly was. Ray's right hand clutched a quilt end, and the hand was trembling. Parson and his wife, DeAnne, had divorced before they'd had children. A blessing, he now saw, because it prevented any possibility of ending up like this.

Martha had not been above lording her family over Parson in the past, enough to where he'd made his visits rare and short. You missed out not having any kids, she'd said to him more than once, words he'd recalled times when Danny pawned a chain saw or posthole digger or some other piece of the farm. It said much of how beaten down Martha appeared that Parson mustered no pleasure in recalling her words now.

He settled his eyes on the kerosene heater emitting its feeble warmth.

"Yeah, it looks to be easier out here all right," he said.

Ray licked his cracked lips and then spoke, his voice raspy.

"That stuff, whatever you call it, has done made my boy crazy. He don't know nothing but a craving."

"It ain't his fault, it's the craving," Martha added, sitting up enough to reveal that she too wore layers of clothing. "Maybe I done something wrong raising him, petted him too much since he was my only boy. The girls always claimed I favored him."

"The girls been up here?" Parson asked. "Seen you like this?"

Martha shook her head.

"They got their own families to look after," she said.

Ray's lower lip trembled.

"That ain't it. They're scared to come up here."

Parson looked at his brother. He had thought this was going to be so much easier, a matter of twenty dollars, that and relaying the sheriff's threat.

"How long you been out here, Ray?"

"I ain't sure," Ray replied.

Martha spoke.

"Not more than a week."

"How long has the electricity been off?"

"Since October," Ray said.

"Is all you've had to eat on that table?"

Ray and Martha didn't meet his eyes.

A family photograph hung on the wall. Parson wondered when it had been put up, before or after Danny moved out. Danny was sixteen, maybe seventeen in the photo. Cocksure but also petulant, the expression of a young man who'd been indulged all his life. His family's golden child. Parson suddenly realized something.

"He's cashing your Social Security checks, isn't he?"

"It ain't his fault," Martha said.

Parson still stood at the foot of the bed, Ray and Martha showing no indication of getting out. They looked like children waiting for him to turn out the light and leave so they could go to sleep. Pawnbrokers, like emergency room doctors and other small gods, had to abjure sympathy. That had never been a problem for Parson. As DeAnne had told him several times, he was a man incapable of understanding another person's heart. You can't feel love, Parson, she'd said. It's like you were given a shot years ago and inoculated.

"I'll get your electricity turned back on," Parson told his brother. "Can you still drive?"

"I can drive," Ray said. "Only thing is, Danny uses that truck for his doings."

"That's going to change," Parson said.

"It ain't Danny's fault," Martha said again.

"Enough of it is," Parson replied.

He went to the corner and lifted the kerosene can. Half full.

"What you taking our kerosene for?" Martha asked.

Parson didn't reply. He left the trailer and trudged back through the snow, the can heavy and awkward, his breath quick white heaves. Not so different from those mornings he'd carried a gallon pail of warm milk from barn to house. Even as a child he'd wanted to leave this place. Never loved it the way Ray had. *Inoculated.*

Parson set the can on the lowered tailgate and perched himself on it as well. He took the lighter and cigarettes from his coat pocket and stared at the house while he smoked. Kindling and logs brought from the woodshed littered the porch. No attempt had been made to stack it.

It would be easy to do, Parson told himself. No one had stirred when he'd driven up and parked five yards from the front door. No one had even peeked out a window. He could step up on the porch and soak the logs and kindling with kerosene, then go around back and pour the rest on the back door. Then Hawkins would put it down as just another meth explosion caused by some punk who couldn't pass high school chemistry. And if others were in there, they were people quite willing to scare two old folks out of their home. No worse than setting fire to a woodpile infested with copperheads. Parson finished his cigarette and flicked it toward the house, a quick hiss as snow quenched the smoldering butt.

He eased off the tailgate and stepped onto the porch, tried the doorknob, and when it turned, stepped into the front room. A dying fire glowed in the hearth. The room had been stripped of anything that could be sold, the only furnishing left a couch pulled up by the fireplace. Even wallpaper had been torn off a wall. The odor of meth infiltrated everything, coated the walls and floor.

Danny and a girl Parson didn't know lay on the couch, a quilt thrown over them. Their clothes were worn and dirty and smelled as if lifted from a Dumpster. As Parson moved toward the couch he stepped over rotting sandwich scraps in paper sacks, candy wrappers, spills from soft drinks. If human shit had been on the floor he would not have been surprised.

"Who is he?" the girl asked Danny.

"A man who's owed twenty dollars," Parson said.

Danny sat up slowly, the girl as well, black stringy hair, flesh whittled away by the meth. Parson looked for something that might set her apart from the dozen or so similar women he saw each week. It took a few moments but he found one thing, a blue four-leaf clover tattooed on her forearm. Parson looked into her dead eyes and saw no indication luck had found her.

"Got tired of stealing from your parents, did you?" Parson asked his nephew.

"What are you talking about?" Danny said. His eyes were light blue, similar to the girl's eyes, bright but at the same time dead. A memory of elementary school came to Parson of colorful insects pinned and enclosed beneath glass.

"That shotgun you stole."

Danny smiled but kept his mouth closed. *Some vanity still left in him*, Parson mused, remembering how the boy had preened even as a child, a comb at the ready in his shirt pocket, nice clothes.

"I didn't figure him to miss it much," Danny said. "That gas station he owns does good enough business for him to buy another."

"You're damn lucky it's me telling you and not the sheriff, though he'll be up here soon as the roads are clear."

Danny looked at the dying fire as if he spoke to it, not Parson.

"So why did you show up? I know it's not to warn me Hawkins is coming."

"Because I want my twenty dollars," Parson said.

"I don't have your twenty dollars," Danny said.

"Then you're going to pay me another way."

"And what's that?"

"By getting in the truck," Parson said. "I'm taking your sorry ass to the bus station. One-way ticket to Atlanta."

"What if I don't want to do that?" Danny said.

There had been a time the boy could have made that comment formidable, for he'd been broad-shouldered and stout, an all-county tight end, but he'd shucked off fifty pounds, the muscles melted away same as his teeth. Parson didn't even bother showing him the revolver.

"Well, you can wait here until the sheriff comes and hauls your worthless ass off to jail."

Danny stared at the fire. The girl reached out her hand, let it settle on Danny's forearm. The room was utterly quiet except for a few crackles and pops from the fire. No time ticked on the fireboard. Parson had bought the Franklin clock from Danny two months ago.

He'd thought briefly of keeping it himself but had resold it to the antiques dealer in Asheville.

"If I get arrested then it's an embarrassment to you. Is that the reason?" Danny asked.

"The reason for what?" Parson replied.

"That you're acting like you give a damn about me."

Parson didn't answer, and for almost a full minute no one spoke. It was the girl who finally broke the silence.

"What about me?"

"I'll buy you a ticket or let you out in Asheville," Parson said. "But you're not staying here."

"We can't go nowhere without our drugs," the girl said.

"Get them then."

She went into the kitchen and came back with a brown paper bag, its top half folded over and crumpled.

"Hey," she said when Parson took it from her.

"I'll give it back when you're boarding the bus," he said.

Danny looked to be contemplating something and Parson wondered if he might have a knife on him, possibly a revolver of his own, but when Danny stood up, hands empty, no handle jutted from his pocket.

"Get your coats on," Parson said. "You'll be riding in the back."

"It's too cold," the girl said.

"No colder than that trailer," Parson said.

Danny paused as he put on a denim jacket.

"So you went out there first."

"Yes," Parson said.

A few moments passed before Danny spoke.

"I didn't make them go out there. They got scared by some guys that were here last week." Danny sneered then, something Parson suspected the boy had probably practiced in front of a mirror. "I check on them more than you do," he said.

"Let's go," Parson said. He dangled the paper bag in front of Danny and the girl, then took the revolver out of his pocket. "I've got both of these, just in case you think you might try something."

They went outside. The snow still fell hard, the way back down to the county road now only a white absence of trees. Danny and the girl stood by the truck's tailgate, but they didn't get in. Danny nodded at the paper bag in Parson's left hand.

"At least give us some so we can stand the cold."

Parson opened the bag, took out one of the baggies. He had no idea if one was enough for the both of them or not. He threw the packet into the truck bed and watched Danny and the girl climb in after it. *No different than you'd do for two hounds with a dog biscuit*, Parson thought, shoving the kerosene can farther inside and hitching the tailgate.

He got in the truck and cranked the engine, drove slowly down the drive. Once on the county road he turned left and began the fifteen-mile trip to Sylva. Danny and the girl huddled against the back window, their heads and Parson's separated by a quarter inch of glass. Their proximity made the cab feel claustrophobic, especially when he heard the girl's muffled crying. Parson turned on the radio, the one station he could pick up promising a foot of snow by nightfall. Then a song he hadn't heard in thirty years, Ernest Tubb's "Walking the Floor Over You." Halfway down Brushy Mountain the road made a quick veer and plunge. Danny and the girl slid across the bed and banged against the tailgate. A few moments later, when the road leveled out, Danny pounded the window with his fist, but Parson didn't look back. He just turned up the radio.

At the bus station, Danny and the girl sat on a bench while Parson bought the tickets. The Atlanta bus wasn't due for an hour, so Parson waited across the room from them. The girl had a busted lip, probably from sliding into the tailgate. She dabbed her mouth with a Kleenex, then stared a long time at the blood on the tissue. Danny was agitated, hands restless, constantly shifting on the bench as though unable to find a comfortable position. He finally got up and came over to where Parson sat, stood before him.

"You never liked me, did you?" Danny said.

Parson looked up at the boy, for though in his twenties Danny was still a boy, would die a boy, Parson believed.

"No, I guess not," Parson said.

"What's happened to me," Danny said. "It ain't all my fault."

"I keep hearing that."

"There's no good jobs in this county. You can't make a living farming no more. If there'd been something for me, a good job I mean."

"I hear there's lots of jobs in Atlanta," Parson said. "It's booming down there, so you're headed to the land of no excuses."

"I don't want to go down there." Danny paused. "I'll die there."

"What you're using will kill you here same as Atlanta. At least down there you won't take your momma and daddy with you."

"You've never cared much for them before, especially Momma. How come you to care now?"

Parson thought about the question, mulled over several possible answers.

"I guess because no one else does," he finally said.

When the bus came, Parson walked with them to the loading platform. He gave the girl the bag and the tickets, then watched the bus groan out from under the awning and head south. There would be several stops before Atlanta, but Danny and the girl would stay aboard because of a promised two hundred dollars sent via Western Union. A promise Parson would not keep.

The Winn-Dixie shelves were emptied of milk and bread, but enough of all else remained to fill four grocery bags. Parson stopped at Steve Jackson's gas station and filled the kerosene can. Neither man mentioned the shotgun now reracked against the pickup's back window. The trip back to Chestnut Cove was slower, more snow on the roads, the visibility less as what dim light the day had left drained into the high mountains to the west. Dark by five, he knew, and it was already past four. After the truck slid a second time, spun, and stopped precariously close to a drop-off, Parson stayed in first or second gear. A trip of thirty minutes in good weather took him an hour.

When he got to the farmhouse, Parson took a flashlight from the dash, carried the groceries into the kitchen. He brought the kerosene into the farmhouse as well, then walked down to the trailer and went inside. The heater's metal wick still glowed orange. Parson cut it off so the metal would cool.

He shone the light on the bed. They were huddled together, Martha's head tucked under Ray's chin, his arms enclosing hers. They were asleep and seemed at peace. Parson felt regret in waking them and for a few minutes did not. He brought a chair from the front room and placed it by the foot of the bed. He waited. Martha woke first. The room was dark and shadowy but she sensed his presence, turned and looked at him. She shifted to see him better and Ray's eyes opened as well.

"You can go back to the house now," Parson said.

They only stared back at him.

"He's gone," Parson said. "And he won't come back. There will be no reason for his friends to come either."

Martha stirred now, sat up in the bed.

"What did you do to him?"

"I didn't do anything," Parson said. "He and his girlfriend wanted to go to Atlanta and I drove them to the bus station."

Martha didn't look like she believed him. She got slowly out of the bed and Ray did as well. They put on their shoes, then moved tentatively to the trailer's door, seemingly with little pleasure. They hesitated.

"Go on," Parson said. "I'll bring the heater."

Parson went and got the kerosene heater. He stooped and lifted it slowly, careful to use his legs instead of his back. Little fuel remained in it, so it wasn't heavy, just awkward. When he came into the front room, his brother and sister-in-law still stood inside the door.

"Hold the door open," he told Ray, "so I can get this thing outside."

Parson got the heater down the steps and carried it the rest of the way. Once inside the farmhouse he set it near the hearth, filled the tank, and turned it on. He and Ray gathered logs and kindling off the front porch and got a good flame going in the fireplace. The flue wasn't drawing as it should. By the time Parson had adjusted it, a smoky odor filled the room, but that was a better smell than the meth. The three of them sat on the couch and unwrapped the sandwiches.

They did not speak even when they'd finished, just stared at the hearth as flame shadows trembled on the walls. Parson thought what an old human feeling this must be, how ten thousand years ago people would have done the same thing on a cold night, would have eaten, then settled before the fire, looked into it and found peace, knowing they'd survived the day and now could rest.

Martha began snoring softly and Parson grew sleepy as well. He roused himself, looked over at his brother, whose eyes still watched the fire. Ray didn't look sleepy, just lost in thought.

Parson got up and stood before the hearth, let the heat soak into his clothes and skin before going out into the cold. He took the revolver from his pocket and gave it to Ray.

"In case any of Danny's friends give you any trouble," Parson said. "I'll get your power turned back on in the morning."

Martha awoke with a start. For a few moments she seemed not to know where she was.

"You ain't thinking of driving back to Tuckasegee tonight?" Ray asked. "The roads will be dangerous."

"I'll be all right. My jeep can handle them."

"I still wish you wouldn't go," Ray said. "You ain't slept under this roof for near forty years. That's too long."

"Not tonight," Parson said.

Ray shook his head.

"I never thought things could ever get like this," he said. "The world, I just don't understand it no more."

Martha spoke.

"Did Danny say where he'd be staying?"

"No," Parson said, and turned to leave.

"I'd rather be in that trailer tonight and knowing he was in this house. Knowing where he is, if he's alive or dead," she said as Parson reached for the doorknob. "You had no right."

Parson walked out to the jeep. It took a few tries but the engine turned over and he made his way down the drive. Only flurries glanced the windshield now. Parson drove slowly and several times had to stop and get out to find the road among the white blankness. Once out of Chestnut Cove, he made better time, but it was after midnight when he got back to Tuckasegee. His alarm clock was set for seven thirty. Parson reset it for eight thirty. If he was late opening, a few minutes or even an hour, it wouldn't matter. Whatever time he showed up, they'd still be there.

SOUTHERN FRIED MASALA

BY ALLY REEVES

Southern Fried Masala:

SNEAK PEAK PUBLICATION FOR BOOK #1
APPALACHIA OUT

WRITTEN AND ILLUSTRATED
BY
ALLY REEVES

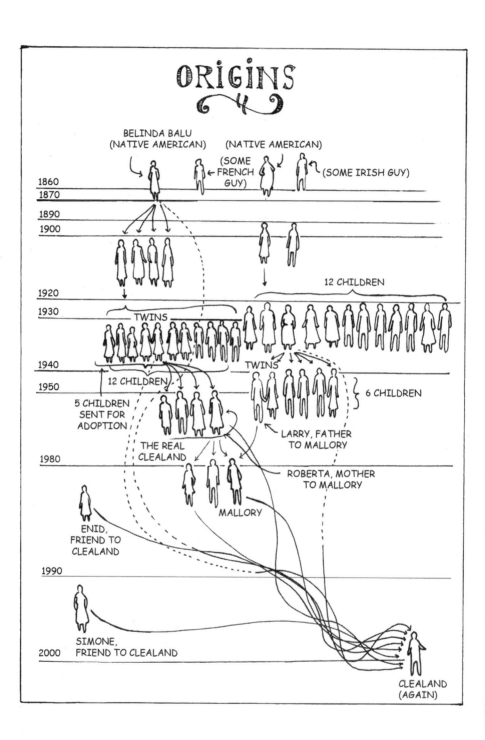

ORiGiNS

ON BOTH SIDES OF THE FAMILY THERE WERE ISSUES WITH MENTAL HEALTH. EVERY FAMILY HAS ITS CRAZIES RIGHT? LIKE ELLA- WHOM i MENTIONED EARLIER. SHE SPENT A COUPLE WEEKS IN THE LOONEY BIN WHEN SHE WAS IN HER 30s....

BUT EVERY FAMILY IS A LITTLE QUIRKY RIGHT?

PEOPLE DON'T TEND TO WANT TO DISCUSS THESE THINGS

BESIDES IT MIGHT BE SOMETHING ELSE LIKE A BAD HABIT BUT NOT MANIA OR DEPRESSION.

THERE ARE SOME THINGS YOU JUST DON'T TALK ABOUT.

FOR EVERYONE'S SAKE.

IT MIGHT JUST BE YOUR BAD ATTITUDE.

IT'S JUST ALCOHOLISM, EXTREME RELIGIOUS VIEWS, OR JUST A STRONG SENSE OF SELF RIGHTEOUSNESS THAT ALLOWS FOR ALL SORTS OF ATYPICAL BEHAVIOR...

LIKE DISAPPEARING SOMETIMES...

SPENDING LARGE AMOUNTS OF MONEY BECAUSE YOU HAVE A SUDDEN IDEA OR SCHEME... ...OR THINKING THAT SOMEONE CLOSE TO YOU IS A PART OF SOME PLOT TO RUIN YOUR LIFE AND REPUTATION...

BUT WHERE WERE WE? THERE ARE SO MANY OF US TO TALK ABOUT AND ALL OF OUR LIVES HAVE ROLLED AND PRESSED INTO ONE ANOTHER. LET'S JUST FOCUS ON CLEALAND FOR NOW...

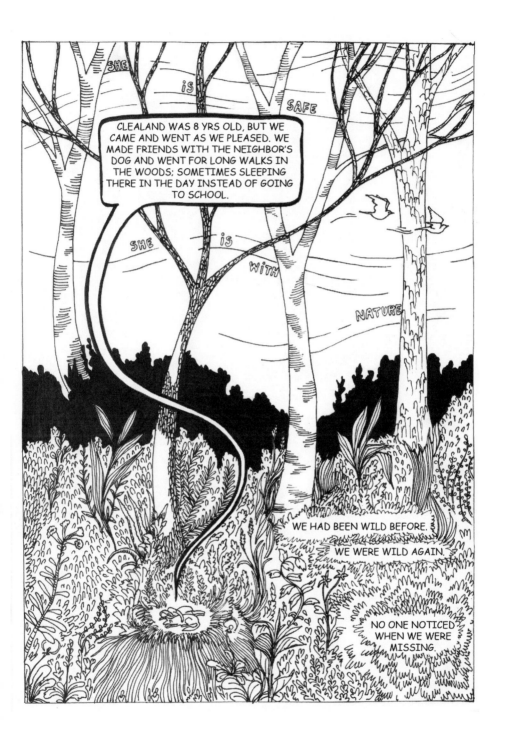

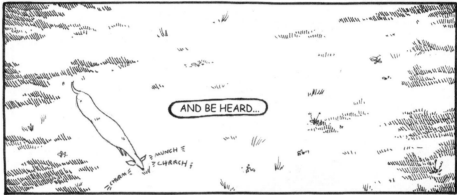

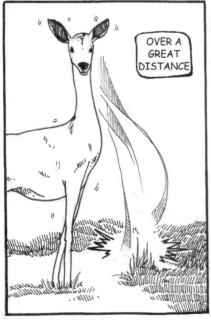

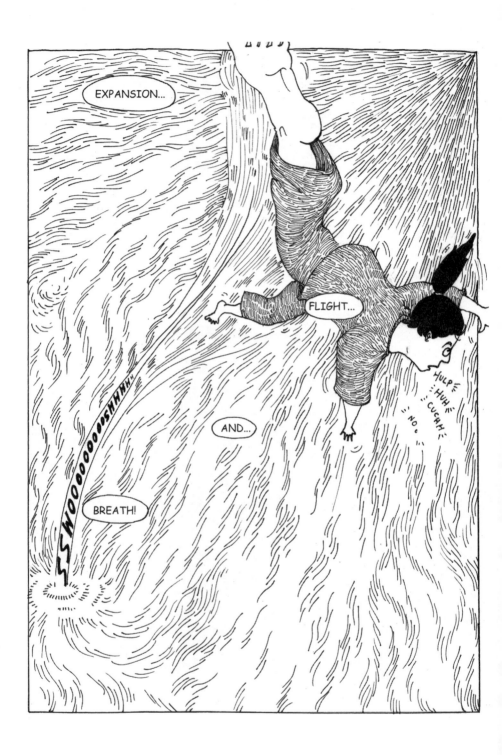

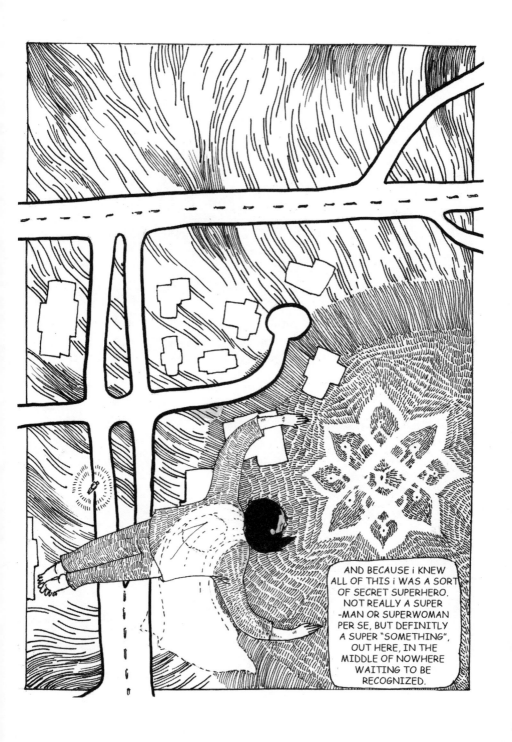

ALLY REEVES

R. T. Smith

The Carter Scratch

What solitude and simmer gave birth
to this sweet mix, one country woman
strumming a duet, melody running
the bass but the up-strings
thumb-brushed for backup rhythm?
It's a mystery how her touch
contrived what's called the Carter Scratch.
Maybe it was mischief in her black guitar.
Maybe the Clinch Mountains are to blame.

Her fingers were deft but leathered
from scraping in the hardscrabble earth
to snatch weeds from the bean vines
and strong as claws from plucking chickens
or shucking the stubborn corn.
She'd heard the river fast over rapids
and smooth at the soothing ford,

so Maybelle rocked in the dark parlor
to raise the cadence—"The Storms
Are on the Ocean," "Bury Me Under
the Weeping Willow." Stitch by stitch,
she improvised an outlaw style, and after
the Bristol Sessions the whisper
talk in Nashville was, "These ridgers
can really pick." She played like sisters

•

and kept her Gibson warm in the kitchen.
Her nails were sharp as talons.
To keep herself busy, she'd sing
and hum and whistle—hymn of the spirit,
skimp and yearn of the stricken flesh—
fret and frail the strings to bliss.
The coffee boiled and corncakes frizzled.
Maybelle called herself a "Nickelsville hick"
and often played at being rapt and simple,

as her nimble hands gave country music
its intricate, quintessential lick.

Bianca Spriggs

My Kinda Woman

for Appalachia

Tall drink of water,
she got a secret
sort of smile.
She got a good voice
and bowed, long legs.
A white father.
A black mother.
Claims Indian roots
somewhere back there,
she's not sure where;
she keep 'em in a closet
full of hooded specters
right next to the boxes
of special occasion lingerie.
She smoke loose leaf,
but only when she drinks.
She drinks only if it's strong
and only if it's sweet.
She can curse and loves hard.
She used to wear Blue
but now it's Red most of the time.
She got dreadlocks, a gingham shift
and a Confederate flag for a belt buckle.
She call her boots roach killers.
A Bible rides around in her backseat.
If you're lucky and she's lonesome,

waiting around for that no-good man,
she might lift her shirt
and show you the scar he left
webbing up her ribs.
She drawls when she's relaxed
and she always relaxed.
She can cook up a storm
when she's happy.
She can smell rain.
Bony in places and hippy in others,
she blushes in Spring
and cackles in the Fall.
She a good old gal,
fine lines and all.

Legend of Negro Mountain

It would take a man black as loam
to have a mountain named for his skin.
Before any highways plaited Allegheny crests,
Nemesis took a bullet in his back while hewing
down clay-skinned men; they parted for him,
felled like saplings before axe and flame.

I know moon-rise, I know star-rise;
        Lay this body down.
I walk in the moonlight, I walk in the starlight
        To lay this body down.

Nemesis was buried in the third eye of the mountain
where his blood had turned the soil black. On this,
the same night he would join his ancestors,

walking trees uprooted from the swamps
he'd been born in. They followed Spica, their branches
raking across the sky and blotting out the stars,
they stayed bad dreams, lost leaves, bark, and limbs,
lost a whole white winter to reach his body.

I'll walk in the graveyard, I'll walk through the graveyard
To lay this body down.
I'll lie in the grave and stretch out my arms;
Lay this body down.

The trees folded constellations into the ground
where Nemesis fell. His ancestors, hauled by blood,
followed these root-walkers from swamp to summit.
And like the trees, they remained—stayed by his body
long enough for a whole mountain to be named
black as a bullet in skin.

I go to judgment in the evening of the day
When I lay this body down;
My soul and your soul will meet in the day
When I lay this body down.

I Would Make a Good Owl

The Owl looked up to the stars above,
and sang to a small guitar . . .
—Edward Lear, "The Owl and the Pussycat"

If I could choose, I would be *Tyto alba*.
The Barn Owl.
I like the look of her face.

•

I think I could live in a tree.
A high, sweet pine.
Or in some cave nook.
Low light.
Plenty of bats.

Instead of arms, I imagine gilded wings
spread across the charcoal night.

Given the right nature,
        I could kill
small, nesting, furred things,

picking their warm, trembling bodies off,
my fleshy talons holding them
with hundreds of times the grip
of the strongest man alive.

Each night, I would hunt, quiet as the moon,
returning to cough up collapsed bones
and pelts damp with digestion
into the mouths of my owlets.

I would be a good owl,
make my way through this world
on a song sung to stars.

Jane Springer

Salt Hill

I was born in a Tennessee sanatorium hours after my mother's father died & I
    know
how the womb becomes a salt-sea grave.

I was born in the last seconds of small crops & small change rained down on the
collection plate's felt pallet & I know

the soul's barn debt to past generations, too.

Outside, ditchfuls of chicory flashed in the after-rain sun as melancholia's purple
scent rose & its steepled fog distilled in Tennessee hills.

& I know I'm not supposed to be here on account of all those crazy aunts & I know
great-grandma was five

when her Cherokee mother died & her daddy dumped her on the red clay curb
of an Arkansas reservation then drove away in a wagon—

how she just strode the fields of milkweed back to Tennessee & married her cousin.

When I was five I drowned a fly in a pie pan of water then spooned it out &
    heaped
a hill of salt on its still body until I could hear a buzz again (as if within a belly)

& I know the rush of the resurrected.

I was born in the last decade of small-town girls wearing white gloves to funerals.

•

As an infant my boy quit suckling long enough to wave to my mother's ghost—
who used to drift in the doorway of the hours.

& at three he told me at my age he had red hair & broke his neck falling off
a runaway horse—I know

        the rocking chair's set too close to the edge of the porch.

What We Call This Frog Hunting

This is the last 2 AM song fit for poling a johnboat through the swamp
so we may glide, quiet enough, to catch frogs with our hands.

It's the year Robertlee can't afford a suit to take me to prom.

Our flashlights tell the difference between alligators & sunken logs
adrift in the dark.

This year Emmyjean's daddy shows us how he guts a deer.

As for the girls, we'd rather be kissing. We've practiced our kissing
on each other—shy as spotted fawns.

We know the boys sometimes meet for a circlejerk in an empty barn.

This is the canvas bag we keep frogs in, once they are caught. It
will hold thirteen by dawn.

It's the year we learn to sew a pleat & stew a coon in Home Ec.

•

T.J. Corbett has such long arms—the boat don't tip when he leans
out over the rim.

This year, we can't all read well enough to fill in class ring forms.

We've never been so aware of skin—the full bag is an organ beating
on the floor of the boat.
                    We barely contain our joy.

This is the year the principal measures the acre between our knees
& the hems of our skirts.

We dock the boat & break the backs of frogs against a stone.

We know they are dead when their tongues unfurl. This is the last
newborn light licked between cypress trunks.

Lunch ladies from here serve fried okra & jambalaya.

The round spot behind each animal eye is an ear—here we circle
the head's globe with a single knife-slice.

Though all year we've swerved to miss guineas by the schoolyard.

We push our thumbs under the edge of skin at the throat to loosen
slick bodies from the green.

This is the year: the dark, the boat, the sunken suits & watery forms,

the catch & kiss, damp canvas, split rib, dawn & entrails in the grass—
we cut the feet last—in the pleated heat—

        then wipe our blades across our thighs & call this happiness.

Pretty Polly

Who made the banjo sad & wrong?
Who made the luckless girl & hell-bound boy?
Who made the ballad? The one, I mean,
where lovers gallop down mountain brush as though in love—
where hooves break ground to blood earth scent.
Who gave the boy swift words to woo the girl from home,
& the girl too pretty to leave alone? He locks one arm
beneath her breasts as they ride on—maybe her apron comes
undone & falls to a ditch of black-eyed Susans. Maybe
she dreams the clouds are so much flour spilt on heaven's table.

I've run the dark county of the heart this music comes from—but
I don't know where to hammer-on or to drop a thumb to the
haunted string that sets the story straight: All night Willie's dug
on Polly's grave with a silver spade & every creek they cross
makes one last splash. Though flocks of swallows loom—the one
hung in cedar now will score the girl's last thrill. Tell
me, why do I love this sawmill-tuned melancholy song
& thud of knuckles darkening the banjo face?
Tell me how to erase the ancient, violent beauty
in the devil of not loving what we love.

Whiskey Pastoral

There were a thousand names for whiskey & only one for joyride
        when the sparkplug stars were supercharged. Only one word
for the cable wherefrom swung the shorn moon.

•

How should we describe the levee scent that was both oil & wool?

After we rolled the jeep into a ditch & climbed out the window
      facing Venus & drew our hands clean down the bent frame's
hill to the valley so deep there should have

been a lake—& after we called for sheep in the dislodged bumper
      & looked down a twisted rubber lane to the undone hood—
we looked for the wolf in a crushed headlight.

Where the stone wall sank low enough that a wolf might climb over
      it, the wheel met the ditch. Where there were wolf-prints, a panel
of steel came apart from the inner workings

of the meadow. From below the dash the radio still bleated: *I'm crying*
      icicles instead of tears & the engine hauled a last bucket of bolts
& washer fluid. The meadow had much going

on we did not understand: The gizmo that opens a window to Lethe,
      the clicker that locks a door perfectly shut, why milkweed pods
explode in late October. Through the back

window our rifles still held in the crook of a rack. What could we tell
      our fathers? We'd have to walk to work. Could it be fixed:
The body soldered & painted to match

previous paint again? Happy accident. Were we herded into the last bunker-
      less pasture for just this: Cobwebs strung blue lyres between long
grasses, while a backseat cooler leaked:

    white lightning
    firewater
    rotgut
    grog

redeye
mule kick
block & tackle
sheep dip—

old tomahawk.

Alex Taylor

A Lakeside Penitence

The old sunken highway. Noon. Wind in the oaks and long spermy clouds leaking over the sky. A kind of dinge to the air and the lake water quiet and gray like pooled grease, the aftermath of hearty cooking. Far ashore, cedars flicker in the breeze. Everywhere the sound of roaming air, of wild lunging atmosphere.

Two brothers, both tattooed, came to this place years ago. In the drear of evening, they stripped to their long johns and, both feeling somewhat buxom with drink, swam to the sunken highway. It had gone under winters ago. Long after it had become defunct of travel, a dike gave way and the lake waters rose and the road sections broke and what remained was a ramp of pavement and loose rebar leaving the shore and going down into the murk. Like a road leading to the frigid nethers of the world.

This was the place to noodle.

These brothers sought out the highway often. Flathead catfish spawned in the crevices and hollows of the pavement. Huge, grizzle-bear catfish, whiskery with age. Pale in the dark fathoms like krakenous ghosts. Talk and rumor floated among the fishermen. The fish below the sunken highway were the size of propane tanks. One was said to have beached itself, a monstrous grandfather, and when its belly was slit open, inside was a stillborn child, something likely tossed over the side of a party pontoon by a drunken teen mother. Other horrors were sure to survive the deeper you went.

But these brothers, Lepshums by blood, were tavern-brave and stricken with brawn from their sawmill jobs. They off-bore crossties six days a week and sported a plethora of muscle. They fished with their hands, chest-deep in water where moccasins and snapping turtles nested, reaching into holes and hollow logs. Between them, they had but sixteen fingers.

Both settled on this afternoon to come to the sunken highway. They were on their way to the burial of a precious and matronly aunt and were already tipsy from prefuneral beers and soap-eyed from crying and they needed a covered dish to bring, casserole or egg salad or something and as yet had nothing, and the road led past the lake and there it was and they stopped and stripped from their trousers and blazers and swam out.

"We'll noodle us a fish," sniveled Doug, the eldest. His face was covered with a mossy beard and he smelled of Brut cologne. "A big one. Cut it up and bring it to the dinner. They can't fault us none for that. And it's what Aunt Vergie would have wanted."

His brother Lum, bald with a barcode tattooed on the back of his neck, strung his belt around his long johns and hitched a stringer of Old Milwaukee to it. The cans bobbed in the water. They made a chimey jingle. It was nice. Such things might save a drowning man. And both brothers were in league against drowning. It was what frightened them most. But they were also in league against being pussies and so would say none of this.

"This is all fine and good," said Lum, wading out, "but we got to remember to go bury Aunt Vergie. We got to try and be on time for once."

Doug waved his concern away, his bare feet easing into the cool bottom mud. "We will, we will. It ain't nothing to wad your Tampax over."

Out at the highway they caught fiddlers for an hour or so, small trivial fish of much bone. They threw these back. Their knuckles were bloodied and they were chin-deep in the tarn, their breath blowing up little squalls. Doug had been finned through the palm and the wound bled like stigmata.

"Well shit," he said, suckling his hand. "I don't hardly believe there's a good fish out here today." His tears had gone away and he seemed freshly saved from a deep impenetrable sorrow. The sight of blood was wont to bring such a reaction from him. It had done so in past times. "We should just go on," he said. "We may be late to the funeral like you said."

Lum looked out over the lake. A jet-ski was scooting over the water, its wake rising white and sudsy. It was piloted by a man in a neon-green life jacket. A red-headed girl rode at his back, the long flame of her hair reaching out behind her like afterburn.

"No. There ain't no good fish out this way. But I don't think we want to run off just yet," said Lum. "Yonder goes some cooch."

Doug looked up. "Where'd they come from?"

"I don't know," said Lum.

Doug, lonely with age, a man who had thrown dog-faced women from his sheets as simply as emptying bed pans, opened a beer and guzzled. "Maybe we should holler them over here," he said. "Get something going."

"Won't be nothing but trouble," said Lum.

"Ain't that all we've ever known?"

True. Both men were accustomed to blights of trouble, week-long benders and broken marriages, but they were ballsy.

"Well, if you don't care to be late," said Lum, "call them over."

Doug climbed atop a piece of highway slag jutting from the lake and waved. The jet-ski turned and roamed over slowly to what appeared to be the sight of some peckerwood distress.

"Everything okay?" asked the man. He rode the jet-ski coolly, his Oakley sunglasses flashing. Behind him, the girl's wet red hair lay tangled over her brown shoulders.

"Oh, we're fine," said Doug. "Just out here doing a bit of noodling. Thought we'd say hello. Hey, that thing there you're riding is pretty nifty, ain't it?" The jet-ski's engine gurgled. On the back, a spear-gun had been lashed to the seat with bungee straps, the barbed harpoon shining.

"It really is a jumping little ride, ain't it?" said Doug.

"It's all right," said the man. "Cost more money than it's worth really."

Doug pulled the empty pockets from his long johns and wrung water from them. Lum crawled toadly up onto the slag and squatted, the four remaining beers dangling from his belt.

"Y'all want a beer?" he asked.

The man shook his head. "Better not."

"Better so," said Lum. "That little piece you got behind you there looks thirsty. But maybe she'd like a drink of something other than beer, reckon?"

The man turned his head the way a spaniel dog might, cocking an ear. "Sir?" he said.

The Lepshums clucked hearty laughter.

"Believe my brother is saying that your girl is cock-hungry for sure. What I mean is she might not really be getting fed the right amount of dick," said Doug.

The jet-ski pilot looked back at the girl. "Do you hear these guys, SheEllen?" he said. "They talk fierce, don't they?"

The girl hid her mouth behind a pruney hand and giggled. "They have problems," she said. "Heartaches."

The Lepshums, pale and lurchish like marooned hogs on their slag piles, gave each other looks. In their wet limp underwear with their stringer of beer they looked like men recently swindled of a great fortune. Or perhaps a misfortune.

The girl went on giggling.

"Is she okay?" asked Doug.

"No." The man shook his head. "She isn't." He lifted the sunglasses from his face and perched them on his head. His eyes were abalone pale. "Neither of us are *okay*."

"What's the trouble?" asked Doug. What at first had been sorrowed randiness had now morphed into genuine concern and he was curious.

"You diagnosed it," said the man. "Not enough dick in my woman's diet. She's suffering from cock-scurvy. I can't seem to rouse a hard-on ever since we lost a great fish out here last summer. It was a huge lunker flathead that snapped my line. When it broke, it sounded like someone had run their fingers over a harp." The man wiped something from his eye. "So maybe you'd like to swim out here and throw the root to her. We're not proud enough to turn away charity. I'll jump off and tread water until you're through."

The Lepshums gave each other counseling stares. Neither of them had encountered folks of this sort before. They were beefy men who rolled hay with razorous women, but here was some kind of proposal, an offer of thighly delights with nothing but water all around to watch. No backseat coupling or billiard room romance had prepared them for this. Their love history was sordid, but contained within its own ramshackle form of decency. They would honeymoon inside a port-o-john were the moment right, but to possess a woman on the back of a jet-ski while her man dogpaddled about as witness seemed beyond them.

They hummed and hawed for a long boring time.

"Let me ask you," said the jet-ski pilot, "you said you were out here for the fish, right? You consider yourselves anglers? Well, here is a real lunker prize." He twisted on the jet-ski saddle and groped SheEllen's thigh. "You might ought to think about hanging a hook in her."

Lum popped a beer and blew foam from the mouth of the can. "We don't use hooks," he said. "We noodle." He held his arms out to show them. "With our hands."

"Your hands?" said the girl. Her face was a flashing bright disc.

"Oh yes, honey doll," said Lum. "We get down in the mire with the fish and just yank them up. Don't use no rod'n'reel."

"Why do you do that?"

The Lepshums considered this.

"I reckon," Doug finally said, "it's because we're just two plain mean-ass sonsabitches." He sneezed and thumbed a long thread of bloody phlegm from his nostrils.

"That's right," said Lum. He nodded proudly. "We don't give a fuck."

The jet-ski pilot spat into the lake. "Well if that's true," he said, "why don't the two of you jump down off those rocks and show us how it's done?"

The Lepshums fell to grinning like boys in the throes of their first whoremongering.

"By God," said Lum. "You two just watch."

He leapt from the slag-pile and floundered in the water before gaining his footing on the sand bottom. Doug slipped in slowly behind him and both were soon groveling at the bellows of the sunken highway. Cheers and applause came from the jet-ski.

They were not long at such trials. Soon, Doug raised up a fish so large and ornery it was like dark fire stolen from the earth's furnace, a great twisting old fish with Fu Manchu whiskers, something that had lain for so long on the lake bottom it had the look of wise sleep in its eyes. It was perhaps three feet in length. Doug lunged and struggled with it and finally climbed atop the slag pile and held it at arm's length by the gills, his face showing stern amazement. He didn't know how he could have missed such a creature earlier, or why only now, at this moment, it was being offered to him.

"That there is a goddamn fish," he said.

And it was. This creature grunted and twisted in his arms, near electric with power. What would save the world were it to ever desire saving.

"One helluva goddamn fish," Doug said. Lum climbed atop the slag-pile and stood beside him and they were together there when the girl on the jet-ski began to squeal.

"I want it!" she said. "Oh, I want it. I want it. It has to be mine."

Her face was almost teary. She slapped the shoulders of her man and bucked and reared on the jet-ski, deep as she was in her wanting throes.

"You heard her," said the man. He'd put his sunglasses back on and was staring at the Lepshums. "Give us the fish."

Both brothers shook their heads. "Woman can't have everything she wants," said Doug. "This fish is ours. We noodled it."

"Give it to us," the man on the jet-ski said again.

"No." Doug held the fish out, its tail whipping up. "This fish will feed our kind, but I don't see the use folks like y'all could get from it. I don't believe folks like y'all have ever had a use for such things. We're going to take this fish to our Aunt Vergie's funeral. We're going to show everybody there what all kind of good we can do."

It seemed a fine speech. Perhaps eulogy for all that the derelict and unfortunate of the world might lose, a pardon-plea for all moral debt they might incur.

"If you were to give it to us, I think SheEllen here would be a mighty pleasant friend to you," the man on the jet-ski said. "Wouldn't you, SheEllen?"

The girl screwed her lips into a squishy smile. Her eyelashes fluttered. "Whoever gives me that fish will be a man that won't walk straight for a week once I'm done with him."

The man turned back to the Lepshums and grinned. "Boys?" he said.

Doug and Lum looked at one another. Then they stared at the woman on the jet-ski, her skin pliant and gleaming, her velvetine aura rippling light and feathery.

"We can't," said Lum. "We lost a good woman. Aunt Vergie. We got to bury her and we need this fish."

Doug looked away from the girl on the jet-ski and into the murky stirred water. "It's true," he said. "We need the fish."

So drunk on grief were Doug and Lum, they didn't see the man on the jet-ski unlash the spear gun and cock the harpoon into place. They were dour and stricken until he spoke.

"For people like us there is no need," he said. "There is only want."

The gun made a kind of sucking burst when it fired. The spear lodged deep in the body of the fish, spilling blood over Doug's legs and splashing it darkly upon the slag-pile, the feathered tail of the harpoon wagging, the retrieval coil leading down into the water. Such was the horror of Doug that he dropped the fish and it fell writhing onto the pavement, and both he and Lum stood mutely numb as the man reeled in the line, the fish slipping off the pavement and into the water.

When it was close, the man on the jet-ski leaned over the handlebars and simply plucked the fish out of the lake and handed it to SheEllen. It lay in her lap and she sat stroking it the way the old and cronish are known to stroke cats. The Lepshums said nothing. They were transfixed like penitents there upon the rocks.

"This fish," said SheEllen, "is better than religion. I feel myself getting lathered." She began panting. The color rose to her cheeks.

"Yes," said the man on the jet-ski. He was grinning up at the Lepshums. "I think it's restored me. I feel ready as a dog with two dicks." He turned and began licking at SheEllen's face.

"Let's get back to shore," said SheEllen. "In a hurry."

The man on the jet-ski wasted no time. He held the harpoon like a jousting spear and turned his rig with his free hand and they sped away, the water geysering up and misting white against the dark of the waiting cedars.

When they were out of sight, Doug sat down on the slag-pile.

"They took our fish," said Lum. "They took it and now we don't have a thing to bring to the funeral."

Doug shook his head. "I guess it wasn't ours," he said. "We wanted it in the wrong kind of way."

Then they were quiet for a long time as the day ended. Just before dark they swam back to shore and drove, wordless and sorrowful, to the burial of their Aunt Vergie, who had already been buried when they got to the cemetery, the graveside service now only pamphlets and tissues blowing about in the breeze and through the gray grass. The grave, neatly mounded, waited under an ash tree. Flowers had been strewn about.

"I think it's good we missed what all went on here," said Lum.

"Yeah," said Doug. He suckled his injured hand and spat blood into the dirt. "We are awful. Plain awful. And we didn't need to see all the kind of good that was happening. We might not of knowed how to take it."

They sniveled for a time, picked through the flowers, but even the fragrance of such blossoms was not enough to hide the recrudescent odor of mud and black water that lay on them, and when they finally left through the iron gates of the cemetery, they left behind them the reek of aged earth and moss and fathoms long in the dark corridors where they had swum.

Now the sunken highway is still there. Drive past it someday and you'll see what it is. It is a span of concrete lost amid dirty waters, the way of all terminal journeys, and it is profitable to consider, just for a single moment, the way we settle into the want of things and that perhaps, given the bitter nature of life, what we are really after is to be stolen from, to be beset by thieves and have all of our struggle end in bereavement. It's lesser and more ignoble things that bring most men to tears.

Jacinda Townsend

Lackland

Meantime, down in Lackland, Lindell was calling on the Lord ever five minutes. It was his first time not sleeping under his daddy's roof up there in Kentucky, and those first few nights in the army's hard bed, he actually cried. Seem like all the kitchen knew how to do was bread and gravy, and while Lindell watched the rest of the soldiers gobble it on down, the gravy looked too mysterious for him to even sniff it. So he just ate bread, which stopped up his bowels. And then there were the army issue socks which bothered his feet something terrible, and he'd be practicing how to wrestle the enemy to the ground when he'd have to duck away from the man he was fighting to itch his foot. Was a piano down in the mess hall, but Lindell was too scared of his T.I. to go over and play it.

'Stead of taking a bath in the water Danaitha boiled on Saturday nights, he had to take showers under cold Lackland water, straddling his poor itchy feet over a rusty drain in the middle of the concrete floor. He always felt the other forty-nine soldiers in the showers with him was laughing at his shrinking balls, even when they wasn't, and the soap the army handed out never really rinsed off, so his feet itched even more powerful. By the time he finally got called up to Mississippi, he done figured out a way to wash his entire body in ninety seconds so he'd have another ninety just to rinse his feet. Lindell'd left Mt. Sterling trying to move hisself to higher ground, but by the time he finished the rounds ever day, he reckoned he warn't the magical Negro he'd thought he was. At night, when he laid in the pitch-black barracks and listened to the boy in the top bunk worm his hips around and spoon out loud through his soup of dreams, Lindell thought he might oughta cut his own feet clean off.

After all he been through in Lackland, he felt like a king when he got on the bus to Biloxi. They'd just built a new barracks and mess hall, and put fancy toys in their electric labs that he couldn't wait to get his hands on. He spent one long night on the bus not asleep but looking out the window at the flattest land he ever seen. No tall trees to speak of— just lone bushes standing like simpletons under the power of the moon. Round midnight, the bus ran longside a train, and on the sides of the boxcars, his mind put movies of all that marching he'd done. It'd started ever morning at 4:30, when the T.I. blew his whistle, and it hadn't ended till ten o'clock at night, when all them soldiers marched theyselves off to the barracks and over the cliffs of hard sleep. They marched to the undersides of jet planes and they marched to the hot gymnasium for push-ups, and then they marched to a clearing where they got down on their bellies and crawled through the mud like gators. It'd got so even when they was supposed to be walking normally, Lindell felt an urge down in his spine to march. Said it made him appreciate Mt. Sterling and the feeling of going nowhere, on account of he ain't never been so tired in his life as he was trying to get somewhere. He was like Jonah, he reckoned—he done got out the whale's belly, but he was all covered in spit. The Force promised less marching in Biloxi, and more time off base at night. They promised shorter mess lines, too, though they ain't promised better food. And they ain't promised not one thing about the White peoples of Biloxi, Mississippi.

Lindell got hisself a right smart interduction to them his first day on Keesler, after he woke hisself up with the birds to go see the ocean. He'd read about the sea in books, so naturally he wanted to see if it was like they said. The sky over Texas had grown his heart right up, with ever cloud what floated by telling him he needed to go pretty places and do front-page things. And there were the words "son, you could be President" bumping around in his head, even if he warn't paying them much never-mind. The Air Force recruiter had told him he was right smart to think of making a doctor, but he'd also promised to send a note up the chain about Lindell trying for army band. Either way, Lindell would put hisself in a bigger life than any other Colored man in Mt. Sterling'd ever let hisself imagine. Seeing the ocean would be just the first of it.

Lindell stretched on his airman's first class uniform and saluted as he walked out the gates of the base and down Irish Hill Drive. It was so early in the morning, warn't even no cars about, and all Lindell could hear was the ocean. The breeze blew right through the gathered legs of his new pants, but it warn't the kind of cold that would upset a body— it was a soft, warm wind like you'd never catch in Mt. Sterling. He'd seen drawings of the sea in his books but he'd never seen it in photographs, and now he still couldn't see the water for all the houses up and down the boulevard, but he could smell how clean it was in the air, how the ocean done took all the dirt of Mississippi far out to sea and left it. He smelt a nothing in the air like he never smelt in Mt. Sterling: everthing the ocean'd washed up to shore, it done already cleaned the night before in its fearsome bowels. When the sun started to make light and Lindell looked at his reflection in the window of a closed thrift shop, he stood up a little straighter and threw his arms out in front of him and imagined hisself leading an orchestra. He could of made his right several times, but the streets was narrow, and anyway he could hear the ocean getting closer, which meant when he finally did make his turn, he'd be right up on it.

He got hisself to St. Francis Street, which was so wide he knew he couldn't walk all the way cross 'thout seeing the ocean, so he closed his eyes.

"Might oughta watch where you going, boy."

Lindell looked, and found hisself standing not two feet in front of a couple of farmers. He knew they was farmers on account of the sun done burnt their necks so red. Their pants were brown, but you could see how they'd been white in some season previous, and sweat had got their collars stiffer'n any woman's starch.

"Where you think you going?" asked the short one. He chewed his tobacco like a cud.

"I'm on my way to the beach, if you'll excuse me."

They both laughed, and Lindell figured by the lack of scratch in their voices that the wrinkles around their eyes wasn't speaking to their true ages—they was young, maybe even young as he was. The tall one wasn't chewing, but he spit tobacco juice anyway, in the sand right next to Lindell's shoe. "Naw you ain't. You ain't a bit more going down to that there beach 'n the man in the moon."

"Must be one of them air monkeys from up North," said the short one. He wasn't smiling anymore, and now he was chewing so hard his nose moved with the force of it. "He don't know we don't *let* Coloreds on our beach."

"You best get your Black ass to base," said the tall one.

The short one winked without smiling and spat again, this time right on Lindell's shoe. They walked on, but Lindell done forgot right then how to move. He stood in the middle of the street so long that a city bus had to slow down, honk, and drive around him—so still that a man in a cotton truck drove a little bit on the sidewalk so as not to hit him. For long about an hour, Lindell just plain couldn't remember how to move. He stood in the middle of St. Francis Street with the waves crashing not a hundred feet from where he was standing, and he heard men shouting at each other while they was searching through the waves for oysters. But Lindell wouldn't look. Matter fact he'd never see the ocean, long as he lived. Turnt out he walked down that street ever weekend on his way to Joe's Oyster House, and he could of just turnt his head a little to the right and seen all that great deep water, but he knew it would of made him just as mad to look as it made him not to. He'd lie in all his letters home, tell Danaitha the ocean was even bigger 'n the sky he'd seen over Texas, but the picture he'd have in his head was from a program he saw on the television.

The Air Force didn't apologize none for the situation, but they did warn him, after the fact, because he got back to base that first day just in time for a special briefing for Negro airmen. It was seven of them, standing out in the hot sun in a straight line, with the sergeant yelling at them through a megaphone like they was a hunderd. They wasn't 'llowed to set foot on the beach, Sarge said, and they wasn't supposed to set down in Whites-only establishments. Sarge yelled out through that megaphone like he was being cut with an ice pick: they was not to be seen riding in a car with a White airman. His voice sounded specially angry right then, and Lindell said he knew it wasn't your regular army angriness, but he couldn't decide whether Sarge hated the Negroes standing in front of him or the rules the White peoples of Biloxi had made to keep them in their place. Lindell looked out the corner of his eye at the six other brothers to see if they was understanding the situation like he was, and sure enough he saw mouths set in "I'll be damned," eyebrows crooked in "what've I gotten myself into." Seven hundred fifty miles south of Kentucky, and Lindell was already in enemy territory. There was rules of engagement the army didn't even know about. Sarge yelled out that the Negro airmen was to ride on the back of the Biloxi buses, and that's when Lindell fixed it in his head he warn't going to be riding on any city buses.

He stepped out for fried okra on Saturdays because he could walk right down Columbus Street to Joe's restaurant, but outside of that, Lindell didn't leave base. He stayed in the rec room and played the two pinball games—KnockOut and Skyway—and he read ever crazy story he could get his hands on through the by-mail book club. He started out with all four books by Claude McKay, and then he found hisself getting more and more peculiar in his appetites, ordering books about monks and priests and even nuns. The light in the rec room was none bright, and Lindell missed the Lexington Public Library with its lamp at every desk, but he figured Negroes warn't 'llowed nowhere near the Biloxi one.

He made hisself quite a few friends, and they never stopped asking him to go see a football game at Our Mother of Sorrows. They just about begged him to get on the bus and go out dancing. "You some kinda queer?" they teased him to his face. "Weird, anyway," they said behind his back. But he didn't never go into town with 'em, not even on the Fourth of July. It got to where he done read all the books about Irish priests and moved on to the American ones. Nobody could beat him at pinball anymore, and the other soldiers liked to just stand by and watch him spin those little wood flippers, his hands rolling from the side of the machine to the front about as fast as they churned over each other on his piano back home. It was other times, after their long nights of carousing the Colored part of town, they'd find him sitting in the room's maroon reclining chair rereading *The Cardinal*, and they'd sit around on the couch and whisper about the thighs of girls they'd met while they watched him speed-read. He was special and unreachable and plenty of fun to watch. Like a dog they could pet when they got back to base.

You might think acting like the sick and shut-in would of kept him out of trouble, but wouldn't you know along come some woman to trip up his stuff. Her name was Marialana, and except for the spread of her hips, she was so skinny she looked like a stalagmite growing out the middle of Joe's restaurant barstool. She had blond hair like honey and blue eyes like a seven o'clock sky, and that kind of buttermilk skin that only other Negroes know is Black. She smoked her cigarettes all showy-like, like she was an actress in a play and the audience had to watch her ever puff to get the story line. Matter fact, that cigarette is what dragged Lindell into her story, because after he reached over the counter for some of Joe's homemade hot sauce, he smelt his uniform burning.

"God Almighty!" he said, and he hopped along the counter holding his hand over the burnt part of his sleeve. Marialana was the only other person there that time of day (Joe had stepped out a minute to buy pickle relish and his wife was home with the arthuritis), and when Lindell looked at her, she held her breath like she was surprised. But smiled at him like she weren't.

"You're on fire," she said, her voice slow in all the wrong places of Mississippi. "You might just have to take that uniform off, cap'n."

Lindell warn't never one to notice a woman on her first try, even if she had elevated his rank, and the more Marialana smiled at him, the more he looked cross at her. "Proper ladies don't smoke," he said.

"Proper ladies?" Marialana asked, still drowning her words. "Who's a proper lady in here?" She giggled into the empty room. "Proper ladies!" she yelled. "Proper ladies! Calling all proper ladies!"

Lindell grabbed her by the shoulders so hard her boobs jogged an inch to the left. He put his face right in hers. "Shut your mouth," he said, but when he looked at that mouth of her'n, it struck him how plump and soft it was, with lighter skin round the corners, like it was filled with sweet cream. He didn't see the pox scar on her chin for looking at the lovely hollow in her throat. He didn't see the tired circles underneath her eyes for looking at the evening pretty of them.

"I ain't a lady," she said. "But I can be your woman this afternoon." She kissed him, and he knew he'd never be able to make a monk. He was long about halfway through his second time reading *The Cardinal*, but right then he forgot ever word. He went home with her, two sandy blocks over, to a house with boards crossing all eight of its windows. Her front porch had sand growing up its sides like it might be sinking down into the Gulf. A man in a white undershirt came out the front door and stood on the porch, and Lindell gave Marialana his arm in case it was her daddy. No woman'd ever liked him so much so quick, and Lindell was thinking it warn't the uniform so much as the man in it. Uncle Sam done toughened him up and smoothed him out like a piece of sweetmeat, and he figured Marialana couldn't even tell he was some hillbilly down off the mountain. They passed the man on the porch, and Lindell opened the front door for her. "Good day, sir," he said, but the man didn't say nothing, just took an empty cigarette pack from his back pocket and crumpled it in his fingers. Marialana snorted. Not a lady, she done already told him, but she was anyways mighty cute.

The wood stairs to her room was scratched up like a hundred bobcats been dancing on them, and it was water beading up on the walls, but Lindell climbed hisself up, past the paint puckering off the banister and the roaches running long into cracks, and into Marialana's tiny single room with a sink and a parakeet in the corner, where he pressed her against the sink and did just about everything he'd thought on doing with a woman for the entire three months previous. Water dripped somewhere in the roof, even though it ain't rained for two days. When they were done, Marialana wiped the lipstick off her chin and squeezed Lindell's cheek. "That's just to make up for the hole in your sleeve," she said. "Next time, I'll need six dollars."

"Six? Dollars? So you're a—a—"

She narrowed her eyes at his stupidity. "Think of it as a token of your affections," she said.

So the next time, out of love, Lindell gave her ten. It was even more than a tithe, since the Air Force only paid him sixty dollars a month.

Lady, prostitute, or otherwise, Lindell wasn't going to do without her. As his weeks went on, he had to halve the money he was mailing home, but he didn't even think twice when he sealed them envelopes 'thout a letter and scribbled out his daddy's address 'thout even so much as a "Danaitha Martin, c/o." He warn't thinking on his wife no more, nor his baby girl, nor a man's responsibility, and certainly not on the Bible.

Marialana done sucked all that up with her creamy mouth. He even took her out for malted milk shakes sometimes after they was finished, just so he could watch her lips wriggle down the straw. Ever time he walked into Joe's Oyster House to find her, Joe'd just shake his head and call "Order up!" to his wife, so she could pop her curler-heavy head up over the window and shake it at the poor bewitched airman. Finally, Lindell's dead mama walked through his dreams to chew him out on a Saturday night. He tried to tell her to leave, but she wouldn't, and when he woke up Sunday morning, he went back to his chair in the rec room and reread *The Cardinal* two times in one day. He stopped going to Joe's. Marialana parked herself out front of the base, but none of the other soldiers would tell her whatever happened to Lindell Wallace. Some of them claimed not to even know him. For love, Lindell took to playing The Lyric's black baby grand in his dreams, so much so that the wood floor next to his bed began to sink under the dream piano's weight. At inspection, when he stood next to Lindell's bed, Sarge felt shorter than usual. Never did understand why.

Well, when I read it in them letters, I got right sad myself, on account of I done spent eight years thinking Lindell was some Negro what flew away from here, and it turns out once he got where he was going, he got his wings clipped just like anybody else—everybody in this town wanting out of it, and ain't not a one of them caring about the fallout. But then I guess there's another way of looking at Lindell's story. His daddy'd always taught him to play by the notes, said if Lindell could only play by ear he wouldn't have no way to tell somebody else how to play his song. But when Lindell looked out on all that Whitefolk mess down there in Biloxi, he probably figured the rules, either way, didn't make any sense. He could've lived on his knees down there, or he could've come back home and died a little inside. The uncooked air in the hallway shifts to coolness and a screech owl rattles out back, and I think to myself what I reckon Lindell thought back then. The important things in life get played by ear.

Jessie van Eerden

Woman with Spirits

We photograph things in order to drive them out of our minds. My stories are a way of shutting my eyes.
—Franz Kafka

Eliza, you sat with Don on the porch swing that the Catholics had built, and you looked at the camera dead center. This was before I was born and before I had my own bout with ambivalence for the place we were from, and for the way I couldn't get my breath sometimes when I left to sleep over at a friend's place in town. Though it happened before I was born, Mom told me that Jessie Beatty Shaffer had told it to her, with a fire in her eyes, insisting that we know because we were Don's relation through Dad's mother if you went back far enough.

Jessie told how President Johnson's photographers came combing through Appalachia in the '60s, trying to capture on film the justification for Johnson's War on Poverty. Everybody in the Whetsell Settlement was furious over how they sneaked in and took shots of your curtained-off toilet, the tobacco juice caked to the floor because Don didn't always use a spittoon, the huge pots for bathwater on the stove, the skinny spigot over the sink that just trickled and sometimes stopped altogether in winter till someone from Beatty Church would take a turn going over to thaw the pipes. The photographers came, Jessie said, and took their pictures, and never asked much about you and never came back.

I came to know you after all that. I rode over with Mom in the truck through both of Butch Mayfield's cattle gates, with applesauce and your mail. Once, during a visit, I handed you a pot holder, wrapped as a present; I don't know why I gave it to you, but I think it had to do with my fear of Don and my shame over that. When we took you and Don to church some Sundays and Don jabbed at the toes of my patent leather shoes with his cane and said things I couldn't make out, he smiled as though it were a game he played and you stood by and shook your head, and I thought he seemed more like your child than your husband.

You stayed in that sloping house for decades, making do on welfare checks that maybe embarrassed you. You stayed even after Butch Mayfield swindled the property from Don for a pittance and left you only lifetime rights to the house, and even after Don died and you were too old to bank your own fires. You stayed even though you knew that an ambulance could never make it up the road to you if you needed it in winter.

You took years of convincing to finally move to an apartment in Kingwood, with carpet and a hot shower. All those years when you lived out the road, I squinted at you with my young eyes and I didn't understand you and I loved the cheap sheer pink scarves you wore on your head for church.

Though I suspect the photographers were well-meaning—reckoning the sacrifice of your dignity small enough on the scale of the greater good—I resent the way they pressed you into the flat, colorless photo and showed you to the world like that. Even as a kid, when I heard about it from Mom, I went out to our swing set and swung and my blood boiled with a resentment that lay beyond my understanding. And, though I need to be careful with my judgments, I admit that I resent the social-service groups who came, too, in their vans—the VISTAs, the Baptist and Catholic kids from the suburbs—talking to you loud and slow, coming to make good for you and assuming that all you knew was squalor. And yet I also wonder sometimes what it was that kept you living out past Butch's two gates for so many years, with a toilet you couldn't flush tissue down, having to burn it in the stove. I wonder if it was habit or stubbornness or love.

I've imagined the scene lots of times. The room would have been so unbelievably still—because you and Don often sat still for a time—that even to fasten a button would be to storm in. And the photographers' Broncos jostled down the rutted drive, past Butch's trailer and the gates, and pulled up to your dark, shingle-sided house (with that blond-wood porch swing smarting their eyes, like a sharp gardenia before a backdrop of tar). And they eased their way in and their shirt collars chafed in the heat and, as you came out to meet them, they said: Could we get you and your husband on the porch, ma'am? (They said that for sure—ma'am.) Could we come in? And later, with fewer ma'ams and more imperatives: Draw the water to heat for your bath, like you just did. Yes, and hold it there. I can presume a camera lens coming in close to catch that rub of Copenhagen in your lower lip. In the top right corner, the lens would catch a framed sketch above the sink, a sketch of Ruth who was a gleaner in the Bible, looking bashful with her ephah of barley there above your sink basins. And then the glossy book came, not with your names printed underneath—Don and Eliza Jeffers—but with captions like: WOMAN AND MAN ON PORCH, WOMAN AND STOVE, WOMAN WITH BUTTER BLACK FROM COAL DUST (a plastic butter dish center-frame, with its lid set down off to the side, and there a black rectangle of butter; then to its left, blurry in the background: a second stove, this one a barreled iron furnace standing as though convicted, guilty of the blackness, its flue not quite flush with the wall as it carries the smoke outside). WOMAN WITH DOG WITH MANGE, WOMAN WITH COAL PILE, and so it would have gone, without you ever meeting that Woman on the page.

You never saw yourself in the way they saw you, framed and cropped for a project. (Through the camera lens, could they have possibly seen the thing you told my mother, when she sighed to you once with a tone of pity, about how you never thought caring for Don—with his mind weakened by a boyhood ear infection even when you first met him in his mother's house—was unbearably hard, because you loved him? And you knew you loved him—even if I just went to the fourth grade, you said, there are still things I know. You said it clearly, and with a hint of reproach.)

Photos expose, but I think this did more than expose. The way Jessie Shaffer told it, with her hackles raised, the photographers bullied you and documented you. It was like they shoved away something, someone pitiable, because then the people who would look might say, Yes, pitiable, and might name you a pathetic name of their own making, shut you up inside that name, flatten you into a photo in a book or a file folder, and the pitiable thing would be outside of themselves, something they could overpower and hold in their hand, at arm's length. They'd tsk-tsk and give money to get you out of there—because, of course, you would need out of there—you and all the pitiable people living in such filth.

But there has to be more to it. I saw you after you moved to the town apartment, where none of the walls leaned in, where the walls were brick. The heat was gas. You had an easy chair, the kitchen sink's silver faucet gleamed. A Scotch-Brite green and yellow sponge sat in its cellophane wrapper on the counter by the sink, and your eyes looked lost, like they'd fallen back into themselves. And you smelled so clean— not a trace of wood smoke.

This thing with you and Don—the way the photographers swept through—it stays with me and works into me now and again, as I move about the world and note the way people look at each other. Sometimes the resentment still boils up, and I am trying to get a handle on it. I took a trip once, in a summer of my early twenties, the first time I ever left the country, my young blood racing. I traveled to Moldova in Eastern Europe to visit my friend Nicole who was teaching English there. I took this trip after you and Don had both died—Don first when they wouldn't release him from the hospital and his heart broke from homesickness and stopped; and then you a few years later in your apartment in Kingwood. This was after I left home for school and after Butch's son Wayne took over Butch's trailer and the two cattle gates.

Moldova is a poor country, hilly farmland mostly, and most of the villages still keep outhouses like the one I was accustomed to at Beatty Church—no crisp flush, the cobwebs and curled dead leaves in the corner. In the cities, the Moldovan women wore heels and skin-tight jeans and eye makeup, but in the villages and towns, I saw simple polyester dresses, kerchiefs like the ones you wore to church, and the people there flashed a look that was familiar to me, a look of learned— and then gradually instinctive—deference mingled with indignation toward outsiders.

The first week I was there, Nicole and I, and her Moldovan friend Valerie, took the small vanlike rutierra to the Orthodox monastery in the town of Hîncu. As the rutierra pulled away, we climbed a dirt path to the monastery: the buildings had been painted a pale, giddy yellow with flowerbeds arranged around them as garnishes. Nuns milled through the grounds, carrying buckets and scrunching up their faces like boys sucking on mouthfuls of sour candies. The backdrop of that pale yellow didn't suit the women; theirs should have been ox-blood black, not a shrill yellow. And we climbed the steps to the main cathedral, entered the narthex where a nun sold pocketbook icons for a few lei, but were turned away in curt Romanian. Nicole translated to me that the floor was being redone and no one could go in that day. So we walked out through the marigold-garnished footpath to a crucifix icon roofed over with an arc of hammered tin punctured in flowery designs. The near-naked Jesus sagged his head left, a dove alighted on his head, a skull and crossbones propped up his nailed-on feet. His eyes rolled back in his head so I could see only the whites.

I was a churchgoing kid through and through—you know that, Eliza, since my family picked you up some Sundays for worship at Beatty. In the pews of my childhood, I studied the bronze, wavy-haired Jesus pictured beside the pulpit and looking off as he did toward the cord that Harold Craig pulled to ring the bell, but looking beyond that, too. I was rabid for Jesus, overearnest and sentimental and enfolded. But, right then in Moldova, thousands of miles from my fold, on the grounds of that monastery of nuns and icons, all whose eyes avoided mine, with my Orthodox-costume scarf askew on my head, a nonbelieving bone all at once rattled around inside me. I decided that this Jesus icon belonged in LaVade Wilson's yard, down from the Gillespies' in the Settlement, next to the other wild things she put out at Halloween, the scarecrow holding a scythe, the plastic Santa lawn ornament wearing a rubber wolf mask. The thought of LaVade Wilson helped me find my footing for a moment, but it wasn't really comfort that I felt.

Nicole and I headed to the outhouse while Valerie waited for us in the shade. After we stuck what was left of our toilet-paper rolls back in our backpacks, we followed the dirt path to the pool where people could bottle holy water, which the nuns also sold along with fizzy water down by the main road. But the holy water spring must have run dry or something since a large off-road truck sat parked alongside it, revving, sprouting a hose that led down into the dry reservoir. A young Moldovan man in dress clothes, looking at our backpacks and jeans, asked in English if we were American and then, without waiting for our reply, said we must stay for the special prayer that was to take place at noon. His dark eyes looked hungry, and though he said nothing else to us, we felt compelled to stay. The rutierra wouldn't come back for us for a couple of hours anyway. We followed the path around to another monastery building where Valerie was waiting, across from the cathedral and LaVade Wilson's sorry Jesus, and we sat together on the steps till noon, watching some Moldovan city women, who'd come on the rutierra with us, pose for photos in their dresses and heels against the pale yellow of the cathedral. And right at noon, the prayer service started within the monastery hall behind us.

It began as a priest's low murmur. Then, at intervals, his Romanian jumped an octave in a shout. We stayed outside on the steps, nervous and quiet, as more and more people crowded in behind us. Soon, and without much warning, the summer day was rent in two by howling and weeping from inside the hall. I could hear a woman, whimpering and shrieking, off and on, in between whatever the priest shouted like a military sergeant giving orders, and I saw the Moldovan man who had told us about the service rush in, shooting us an eager glance. After a while, Valerie told us in halted English that it was an exorcism and that the woman had come for prayer and the priest was ridding her of a spirit. Valerie shifted her weight till she finally went in because she wanted to see it. Nicole and I sat as though pinned to the steps, with nothing to look at but the Jesus icon under its tin roof, and I shut my eyes.

But, Eliza, I didn't shut my eyes because all of this was foreign, though I knew the Moldovan man didn't assume an exorcist past on our part. Instead, it held an eerie familiarity. It was pushing me to understand something, but I didn't know what exactly. I knew that as a little girl in the Settlement, I'd heard the story of Christ casting the unclean spirits out of a man who roamed the caves and cut himself with stones. Jesus sent the demons out into a herd of swine, and I knew a couple of people who tried to follow suit—like the Beatty pastor, the Reverend Joe Gainer, who wouldn't wear glasses because he believed God would heal his eyes. He came once to the hospital when my brother Luke had encephalitis and was sick with seizures, and the man tried to exorcise Luke, right there in the hospital room, till Mom asked him to leave.

And one summer, my two brothers and my sister and I listened wide-eyed as a demon was cast out of a girl over the radio. We were teenagers, and every day that summer, we tuned in to Bob Larson's radio show *Talk Back* that came on at two in the afternoon on WAJR. On the girls' side of a long upstairs room that we all shared, we huddled around the single working speaker of a hand-me-down stereo that Uncle Todd had brought us from Ohio. We'd heard about Larson from Barry Shaffer, the evangelist who preached the chapels that year at Aldersgate Camp up in Cranesville. Barry was from Pittsburgh and he'd brought some Pittsburgh kids to the camp, girls who wore makeup and threaded their fingers through their hair and dropped their jaws at the camp's outdoor bathhouses. And Barry ignited us when he preached; he rallied in us what we called a work of the Holy Spirit but what also gave us a sense of self, a kind of access to a spiritual power that we could wield in a world in which we were a bit scruffy and insignificant. An actual world in which we received, not a fierce laying-on-of-hands, like Barry talked about, but a hand-me-down stereo from our uncle who had money in Ohio.

As Bob Larson took his callers, we assumed positions of the stunned devout: we lay on our stomachs, clenching a bed pillow; we hugged our knees and leaned against the attic door. Larson mostly preached against Satanic cults and rock music and asked for money. But he had us rapt; he had a voice that raked through our minds, snagging on a knot of doubt now and then, and it hurt when he pulled at the knot because he had bravado. He had sugary pity (for the weepy callers) and fiery, righteous anger (for the lost callers in denial). And he had us hanging on his every word.

When Larson got the call from a girl possessed with a demon, we went rigid in our young bodies. She whimpered into the phone about rape and beatings and then started wheezing and, in a weird voice, she made throaty death threats, which never cowed Larson—he shouted back at the girl, and the static over the phone lines or in the speakers crackled like fire, and he did battle with her evil spirit right there on the air. He named the spirit Legion because he said there were many in her, tormenting her, he said in the name of Jesus, in the name of Jesus, leave her, and the girl yelped and she came out of it with a weak, puppy voice dripping with gratitude and tears, as he kept stroking her with his voice, promising her pamphlets in the mail and his newsletter. Larson came out of it with a few donations to the show.

I faced the stereo speaker and shut my eyes tight, imagining this girl who seemed like she would have pale, bluish skin, papery skin that showed every bruise, and she glistened with sweat and sat alone and held her own hands.

Jess, Jake said to me, you don't have to be afraid. You're a believer. But he didn't sound convinced himself—we were small and defenseless in our upstairs room, still listening as an ad came on. I was afraid, but I wasn't as afraid as I was longing to know who the girl really was, what she looked like and why she'd called in and if, when she hung up the phone, she cried, or sat still, or what. Larson took another caller, someone abused by Satanists, someone who said he had eaten a ceremony victim's heart—which segued into a pitch for more money—then someone hosting another band of demons, someone calling from a shabby room with a single-bulb light.

I remembered this girl's radio voice when the shrieking and thrashing started in that Moldovan monastery, in the hall behind me, and I remembered you, Eliza, and it was that same resentment that I felt. Anybody could tell by the woman's screaming that she suffered. And anybody could tell that the priest's voice was raking through her, in the heat of incense and icons, with prayers in a tongue I didn't understand but with a merciless force I knew something about. And, Eliza, she was defenseless and, in that crowd, she was alone.

I have tried, these past few years, to find those pictures they took of you and Don. I've searched in books and archives and libraries, but never found them. The closest I came was a photo taken in 1935 in Terra Alta, up on the mountain a few miles from where we lived. I found it in this magazine, *Art in America,* and the article said the photo was taken by Walker Evans who was one of FDR's photographers commissioned to drum up public support for Roosevelt's New Deal during the Depression by taking pictures. In the photograph, a girl wearing a middy blouse with puffy sleeves and a sequined party hat reaches out her hand to touch or point to something outside of the photo's frame. Beside her is an older, shorter woman wearing a heavy coat with a fur collar (even though it's July), and she's clutching a tissue or maybe a coin purse to her chest. The article said that on July 4, 1935, New York photographer Walker Evans entered Terra Alta, West Virginia, and during the town's festivities, photographed these two women and, thereafter, filed their faces under his name in the Library of Congress as "Independence Day, Terra Alta, West Virginia, 1935 July, gelatin silver print." Evans helped give American poverty a visible face, said the article, but in his diary on the day he took this picture, Evans wrote:

> In end of rain to Terra Alta pronounced Teralta. There a homecoming of natives, very degenerate natives, mush faced, apathetic, the pall of ignorance on all sides. Photographed the most gruesome specimens.

I read and reread what Evans wrote and I felt again that resentment, even fury. I'm not foolish enough to deny the marks of the poverty of that time—the marks even remained when I was a girl in the '80s spending every July Fourth in Teralta at my Aunt Becky's along the parade route. It was a railroad town and, of course, the railroad boom had shriveled to a joke. Across the street from Becky's place, a house lined its railing with fake flowers and propped up its porch roof with two-by-fours. I remember that it always rained, and I loved the rain, and I felt love for that place. But even if I hadn't gone there as a little girl and felt a particular pride, the fury would still rise up—and that fury is becoming clearer to me—because, commissioned as he was, Evans wielded his camera with a power that the people in front of his lens didn't have. He framed and cropped their suffering, forced it into a black-and-white record, and claimed for himself a private knowledge of them—that violent kind of knowledge that says: I own you, I clutch you like you clutch that coin purse, there is nothing new or strange in you that I don't already know and haven't already risen above, there is, in fact, no bloom in you, and it's a pity. He gave no thought to the middy-blouse girl's mind as a thing layered like an onion, like a rose. He did not accord her the weeping and the exulting, the prismatic experience of sunlight that Evans certainly maintained for himself in his own complexity. He doomed the girl in the middy blouse and party hat and, by doing so, drove her out, away from him, left her alone, and at the same time, he drove out his own vulnerable fear that he may have had about things falling apart, the world falling apart and meaning being lost, and about how he might as well turn to the wall when that happened.

President Johnson's war started when the poverty of the '30s rusted into the poverty of the '60s. In 1964, Lyndon and Lady Bird Johnson climbed onto a sagging porch in Inez, Kentucky, and in front of TV cameras he said: "I have called for a national war on poverty. Our objective: total victory." And the photographers again went searching, in shacks and slums and down roads with two cattle gates, to find the poor and shove them into the light for the others to see and make claims on. To shove people onto a path of redemption, of clean carpets, hot showers, huge-pipe sinks, and silent, well-ordered rooms.

Eliza, you had a single-bulb pantry, with a narrow window, before you moved to Kingwood. It was a pretty pantry, I remember, you said so yourself. Liz Sisler, when she went to work for the Senior Center, came over from her house a couple of miles away, and helped you put contact paper on all the shelves to put the canned goods on, and also some of those old Ball jars of blue glass, overturned and beautiful in the window light. The contact paper was white with tiny purple flowers in three different phases of blossoming: bud to full-face to bending and bent with petals closing up. The pantry walls leaned toward the center from the weight of split firewood stacked against the other side of the wall. You finished it before dark, so Liz could make it back home for supper, down the hill a ways, down her driveway pocked like a dry riverbed, her chickens loose among the ducks.

If the photographers would have come again, they might have made that picture of you in your pantry not very full. And who would have been able to tell the purple of the flowers or the blue of the jars in a black-and-white picture, and who would have known that Liz had helped and that you had listened to music on the radio while you worked at it, and that there were days you spent, when it was warm in the sun by the window, arranging till they suited you the canned beets that people in the Settlement gave you, and the soups and the beans. The team of photographers might still have assumed your apathy, your ignorance—but then, I am not being careful with my judgment. I am speaking out of fury, knowing that fury can have the same source as love. And I am still learning how to temper them both.

All that is to say, when the Moldovan woman in a kerchief and a simple polyester housedress, this exorcised woman followed by a throng of other kerchiefed women, carried her cries outside of the monastery and sent them up against the pale yellow of the shut-up cathedral's outer walls—I felt fury and no longer nervousness. I was furious with the priest's strong-arming, but also somehow with myself, how I just sat there.

She lay on the floor of the porch and flopped like a hurt fish until she went limp. All was quiet and she just twitched now and then, till someone from the crowd took her arm and led her away. The priest was nowhere to be seen. I never did get a look at him. All of the other winded believers slowly shuffled past LaVade Wilson's Jesus, crossing themselves. And all throughout the exorcism, over by the cathedral, those women in heels kept posing in front of the yellow, in a Marilyn Monroe forward bend, grinning despite the shrieks.

So, the man in dress clothes came over and said to us on the steps, nodding toward the porch where the woman had fish-flopped, if you don't see this, then you don't believe. And he brushed his hands together, as though just finishing a job.

That's not true, I actually said, fuming beyond reason, foolish and wanting to say something sensible about what had happened, that there had to be more to it, but he wasn't listening. He was crossing himself mechanically in front of the same icon that I had begun to hate for its grasp on the people who passed by it.

The woman's howls, still hanging in the air, were like imagined things in my mind. The howling was supposed to be the sound of the demon as it left, an evil spirit driven out, flapping its monstrous wings and fleeing—like Legion leaving the girl who dissolved into drivel on the radio at the command of Bob Larson.

I remember the remaining shell of the exorcised woman as she trembled and faltered on the monastery's footpath, and you, Eliza, come into my mind, vivid like a vision, though not fiery. Just clear. I think of you offered up to the camera, as to a priest—undefended—subject to the lens peering in, and it's as though someone said, with smugness: I know all about your soul. The photographers, the priests, they look at a face as if by looking they can grasp and know—they name the demon and cast it out, they frame the guilty stove and the pouched lip in a photo and call it poverty, call you poor, call the sorrow Legion, and purge it all out, but there is more blooming there than they can ever know.

A sadness still shook the kerchiefed woman whose demons had already up and fled, but we all, on the monastery's porch, cowered from it. Someone had presumed the woman needed a priest's prayer and holy water, just as someone presumed what you needed, urging you toward a move to town, to a hot shower, even when you said, I've been sponge-bathing for seventy years, why would I need a hot shower now? Even when you could mourn Don in that shingle-sided house in ways you couldn't anywhere else, in that place where your curtain-walls hung and smoke worked into the folds of cloth and skin.

I have, I guess, no dread of demons, though I once did. I do have dread of our mishandling of one another, and the shoving we do of one another's souls as though our souls were clods of dirt—how we can abandon one another to our sorrows, shut one another up into it, though we do it with great shows of helping, always with these great shows and programs and prayer services and claims on redemption. Maybe our abandonment is most frightful when veiled by these compassionate shows. Might it be that when you hurt, something in you opens, and the pain takes root and takes prominence, and if I allow it its root, acknowledge it in you, and come to you powerless, with no commands, and sit with you if you want me to, something in me might open, too, some fuller dimension of your private suffering?

A small girl walked by Nicole and me as we sat on the steps of the monastery. Over her little energetic body she wore a rust-red skirt and magenta top. The mismatched skirt-set hung a bit loose. Maybe hand-me-downs. She moved without shyness; she moved with her whole self. When she looked right at me as she stole past, I was finally able to cry. She held something stubborn in her—running like a lion down the path—something discordant and strange, with some quality in her soul that refused to be known. I was sick for home and sick for this girl's defiance—it was there in you, too, there despite it all—defiance toward anybody's pronouncements, toward even a written portrait that, in its best effort, is still a kind of containment, failing in the face of your resistance. And it's good that it fails. I just wanted to write you, to tell you, that I don't need to find those photos to see you.

I can shut my eyes and see you, beyond the edge of a photograph. The deep rut lines on your face full of coal smoke, your hands gone soft ever since you couldn't lift the firewood. Your nails that Liz sometimes painted. The crevasse of both worry and welcome between your brows. Your bent back. Your secret light stealing now and then across your eyes. The syringes and the SSI checks and the half-eaten cup of cottage cheese on the table all insisting: I'm here. I shut my eyes and see your yellow AM/FM radio, its antenna straining toward the window like a gladiola stem, and you hold the shabby thing in your hands and look at me.

Charles Dodd White

Controlled Burn

Sheriff Gene Wilcox had the decency to drive up to the ridgeline where we were breaking ground on the new development to tell me himself of the government's coming crime. I'll hand him that. There are other men who would have sent a deputy. More generous man than me might call that kindly. But I've never been a friend to those that pin a badge over their hearts.

He pulled his unmarked Crown Vic up to the tail end of the zig-zagged ruts where the bulldozer sat idle and cut his engine. It was the lunchbreak and my Mexican boys were off under a shade tree eating their tortillas and menudo. My feet were propped on my old Igloo cooler, tall boys of Old Milwaukee and Pabst sweating inside. It was getting on to that time of the afternoon when cracking one open would be a shame worth bearing.

He hauled himself out of his cruiser and threw his hand up and I told him to come on and grab him a seat. His guts ballooned when he eased his carcass down on the chair, the aluminum legs groaning and digging little wellshafts in the sand.

"You ain't gonna care for this, Dayton," were the first wicked words out of his mouth.

"Wanna sip of something?" I ignored him, toeing the cooler.

"You got Co-Cola?"

He read the look on my face like he'd chalked it there himself.

"I guess I'd better not then."

He sat there passing a penknife over the white rims of his fingernails, shaving air, killing time.

"Well?" I asked. "I know you ain't up here to ask how high my corn patch is standing."

He tore a shred of hangnail and spilled some of the breath he'd been catching.

"It's your Daddy's place, Dayton. The tract up there above Parson's Den. They've found something."

"They?"

He spat dryly.

"FBI. Called me up there to have a look just this morning."

I popped the cooler open and dragged my hand through the ice for the first can I came across. I could feel my fingers turning baby pink from the cold.

"You're about two months too late for April Fools, Gene."

"I wish that was the case. I surely do. But this is serious."

I looked over his shoulder at a pair of turkey vultures turning in the haze, their clockwise circling seeming to screw down a big lid of hot air over all the greenly slumping mountains. There was some kind of old-fashioned peace in it.

"Some bastard had him a weapons cache up there," he went on. "One of these end-of-the-world nuts. A postman or some such. Booby trapped the whole thing with dynamite and trip wires. Hell, with as much as he's supposed have stuck up there, it's enough to blow the top of the mountain off. Government wants to burn it out. Do a controlled burn. Dig firebreaks between the ridgelines. That way they can keep from hauling it all down and risk having it blow up on 'em."

I took a drink of the Pabst. It passed down my throat like a sad song going back the way it had come.

"What about my Daddy's old hunting cabin?"

He studied the silent black tongues of his shoes.

"It's on the wrong side of the creek, Day. There ain't no way to save it."

"Well," I said. "I guess I won't be taking your word on that."

After he'd left, and once I put my mind around what Gene had said a good long while, I had the Mexican boys knock off early and pile into the truck. Most of them rode in the back along with the rattling gear. My head man, Ernesto, sat up in the cab with me, smoking a Benson & Hedges.

Most of the Mexicans got off at the crossroads, but I drove Ernesto up to his place, the illegal trailer park out behind the back of the elementary school in Cullowhee. His family lived in a beaten box that looked like something that had fallen out of the sky and been kicked across the yard by a mean kid. Wasps jerked back and forth through broken windows and stove-in walls. A brown woman stood over a pair of babies in diapers and matching yellow T-shirts. If she had of been twenty pounds lighter, she might have been something to look at.

"I guess you wouldn't be interested in making some extra dollars this weekend?" I asked.

He stared out the windshield at all that heat, the yard grown up with tall blond weeds, seeing something other than that pitiful excuse for a homeplace for him and his family. Few men I've known can look on the sorry truth of something and admit it's as bad as it is, even if the admitting is to themselves alone.

"You want help with your father's cabin," he said, breathing out lung smoke.

"That's right."

He shook his head, not looking me in the eye.

"That cabin's going to burn, Mister Dayton. Didn't you hear what the sheriff said? Too dangerous. You should never think the law will allow you to do such things."

He pitched his butt out the window and swung the door open.

"Be careful, Mister Dayton," he said, walking on up to his trailer, putting his flat hand in the air to say goodbye.

I stared up at his little rotten trailer on the hill for a while, then drove the truck back out on the rutted drive and headed to the hardtop. I sat there and smoked a cigarette before I decided to ride up to Lookout Cove, going on to what everybody now called Tommy's place.

When I cut the truck's engine there was nothing but a mountain of quiet in that yard. Seemed to be empty at the big house. I sat there and remembered how the place had taken shape under my hand more than thirty years ago. Remembered too the year Martha, the boys, and me had wintered in a kerosene-heated lean-to while I dragged the house's timbers into their proper angles, pulling something like a home up out of the ground.

It was nearly five years since Martha had died, leaving the place so lonesome and gutted out, nothing but the ghosts of our now-grown children running around on those moaning floorboards. I'd been happy to sell it to Tommy and move downcountry a ways. My trailer and cats were about all I could take at the time, and besides, Tommy seemed all set on starting a family, fathering his own passel of boys. But, of course, all of that has come to nothing.

When I got out I could hear the garden hose spray around on the side. I knew that would be my son's wife Maybelline, tending her tomato and okra patch. She is one hell of a good-looking woman, blonde headed and deep through the curves. She wore cutoffs and a tank top sucked tight to her chest. In her hair she had a blue bandanna wrapped up snug. If I had of been Tommy, I would of put a softer shape around her middle years ago.

I said hello and flirted with her a bit. She smiled and told me Tommy was around back. I went around and found my son on the screened-in back porch, the door propped open, letting every description of mosquito into the place. He leaned over a vise locked down on an upright fishhook, tying flies. I'd never once lifted my hand to cast a fly rod. Never saw the fish in any of these mountain waters that a spinner reel and a piece of corn wouldn't catch just as good as any such fancy rig. But Tommy'd picked up the hobby from some of those Asheville hippies he's been known to run with. Hell of a man for expensive habits that have nothing to do with the way he was raised.

"What brings you up, Daddy?" he asked, not looking up from his magnifying glass and blunt scissors.

"Just driving through is all."

"That right?"

"It is."

"You wouldn't mind a drink of something, I bet."

I allowed that I wasn't allergic. He tipped back in his chair and opened the mint-green door on a fridge the size of a TV. He tugged out a couple of Budweiser longnecks, popped the caps and handed one to me.

"It'll beat a summer day," I said, grateful for the chance it gave me to think. It was a while before I got around to what I'd come up for. "Actually, son, there is something."

"Course there is."

"You don't have to say it like that."

"How you want it said, then?"

"Like nothing, Tommy."

We drank and watched the mosquitoes drift in and light on the backs of our hands, flexing their slim checkered legs before we'd take a swipe and they'd swirl off, just to do it again in another couple of seconds.

"I need your help, is all. There's a controlled burn being laid down up on Parson's Den. If we don't do something, your Grandaddy's cabin won't make it."

He smiled down at the tops of his sandals and pinched the bill of his Duke cap between his fingers.

"I thought that old place ruined years ago. It's got to be eat up with termites."

"It ain't that bad."

"Bad enough, I guess."

I knocked back the rest of the Bud.

"Well, I ain't asking for your charity."

I started to leave.

"Don't go running off," he said, standing up. "When you need me, Daddy?"

I very nearly told him to go to hell. Very nearly.

"First thing Saturday morning," I said. "Make sure you've got your chainsaw and some bar oil."

He snapped the bottleneck up from between his veed fingers and sucked on the glass.

"Bring some coffee, will you?" he said.

I was up before the chickens. It's been that way since Martha passed on. Never can sleep through the early hours of the morning. Too much haste in a man's life when he has as little time left as I do.

I went on to the kitchen and put a can of Kozy Kitten on the electric can opener. As soon as it started turning, I had cats dripping off every chair and table in sight. I plopped the pale mealy mess out onto half a dozen pie plates and let the brats set to it, their purring so loud I could hear it above the Mr. Coffee.

"Eat up, fatbodies," I told them. They meowed back.

It was just light when I pulled up to Tommy's place. He was already out on the front stoop, his gear piled up in a little tower. I left the truck running while I got out and helped him stash everything in the bed. I smoked a cigarette while he sipped from my thermos and then we went on.

I took the 107 up past one of the gated communities near Cashiers. I'd helped build all those places up there nearly a decade back. Once we were down on the opposite side of the creek with the road flung out, we could see up to the distant ridges, each of those big houses stuck to the side of the mountain like flying saucers that had crashed there and been left stranded. The big glass A-frames shone like grit in sand.

"A damn shame," Tommy said, his mouth loose above the black plastic rim of the thermos.

I glanced back at the development.

"What's that supposed to mean?"

"Just me talking. It doesn't mean anything."

"The shit it don't."

"Watch your blood pressure, Daddy."

We drove for a piece.

"I guess you're forgetting all them houses up there is what paid for your college. Paid for that house you're living in, too. Your Momma sure as hell never had a problem with it."

"No, Daddy. I'm not forgetting any of that."

We pulled off at a station a ways up to top the gas. From there on all the way up to my Daddy's place, we didn't trade a word.

I took us into the property through the back way. The main route was blocked off by the government to keep campers and hikers out of their planned hell. The dirt drive was carved deep from the weather and the years. It was tight with overgrowth, branches and vines slapping the windshield and the top of the cab. Caught limbs scratched up from beneath the truck's floorboard. I could feel it through my boots, a dull uneasiness on the soles of my feet.

"You remember turkey hunting up here?"

For a long time I didn't think he was going to answer me.

"Yeah I remember it," he said. "Seems like another life."

"It does, well enough."

Once we got up to the cabin I pulled off on a hard gravel bank on the high side of the property. It was cool under the shade trees and not too buggy. A little creek that never carried a name floated by. It never had been anything to anyone, and still wasn't much more than a dimple through sand flats. From where I was standing, I could see clear to the smooth bottom. It was only a matter of a few inches from the surface to the bed. But still I could remember how it had been there for all of the fifty-two years I'd been coming up, running a course as regular as a race-track, always scant and shallow, never digging a place for itself in the sediment. I wondered how that could be. How a stream could bleed itself down through the years without making some scar on the earth.

I went on to check the hunting cabin while Tommy brought all the gear down front. It had been near two years since I'd stepped foot in the old place. The door had come loose at the top hinge so that the board was jammed until I lifted with all I had and swung in. Inside it was dank as a grave. Spider webs hung from the roofbeams, going silver and trembling in the sudden gush of sunlight. I put my hands out in front of me, running the webs through with the ends of my fingers. The webs clung. I went back out and clapped and dusted my hands until I got the whole cloudy mess off. Tommy didn't offer to lift a finger.

Once our gear was settled, I showed him what I intended. We needed to cut away as much high-standing timber as we could, reduce any fuel the wildfire might find as it came close to the cabin. Tommy brought his chainsaw out and we started felling every tall tree around the place, laying the fat and skinny trunks alike with great booms against the ground. I'd spell him occasionally, though there wasn't much hard work in what we were doing. Not with the big orange Stihl notching angles on the trunks and gravity doing the rest. It was something else to see those trees chewed up like that, vines ripping from the top branches on the way down like wigs being snatched off the heads of dying women. By early afternoon we'd cut a good perimeter fifty feet deep in every direction. We sat down on the cabin's porch and ate what we brought with us, looking on the country we had just opened up.

"You think that's far enough to keep the fire off?"

"We can only pray," I told him.

That night we sat up on the porch and watched heat lightning shake itself loose somewhere far out in the dark, hoping it would turn into rain, but it never did. Under that sad sky I remembered the nights I'd sat out there on that very spot as a boy and listened to rain snapping on the tin roof like gunshots. Could still see the way my Daddy and his hunting buddies would holler and carry on, telling lies and helping each other to their bunks when they'd gone and got stumbling drunk. It was scribbled down deep in my brain to become the kind of man my father was. But something had happened in those years in between. Looking at Tommy I could see it, as plain as plyboard. A space between the two of us had grown up that no matter of talking or sitting would ever change.

I don't remember making my way to my bunk and falling asleep. Only the gray light throbbing at the edges of my eyes the next morning and Tommy standing over me, a pair of coffee mugs in his hands.

"They've set it," he said.

I swung my feet down and shook out my boots in case a scorpion had nested in them overnight. I could smell the smoke, sharp as daylight.

We walked on out to the yard and looked down the mountain. We couldn't hear anything yet, only see the smoke coming on through the trees like true evil given shape.

"Hell of a thing to do on a Sunday," I said.

He gave me one of the coffees. It was pure heat in my hands. We stood there until the sun was full up, the smoke moving on its own sick yellowed tide, the backlight of daytime making the trees seem to smolder before the fire had even reached them, an illusion out there amongst things I thought I knew. Once I'd bottomed the mug, we could hear flames faintly cracking.

The fire, the bigness of it, was a monster coming to this world like true hate. Birds flew past, carrying the smell of scorch. I moved out there with Tommy among the felled timber of our fire break, waiting for the great wrecking to come, the entire measure of whatever unnatural force those men had put in motion. The sky was blue that morning, blue and endless. But when the smoke came, the color drew back. There was only the smoke, and me and Tommy standing in the middle of it, knowing the land was giving up on all of us.

The explosions came from far down the hill, a good half a mile off. Even so, the first detonation sounded like the earth's spine had been jerked up and snapped clean in two. Then, nearly a minute later, the secondary explosions went off in a regular chain, dull and sharp alike, the stockpiled bullets and dynamite cooking off, shaking the ground beneath my feet. It was enough to make Tommy sling his coffee out on the dirt and begin loading gear in the truck. After another few minutes of watching the smoke come on, I started helping him.

It's hard to say when I saw the first of the fireline. The smoke was a strange mirror, bending everything around so that what I saw may have been with my eyes or my head. But when I could feel the coming heat on my face like a sunset, I knew we had to leave.

Tommy was already sitting in the truck with the engine running when I headed up. I got in and he pulled off without a word. We kept the windows rolled up and the air conditioning off to keep from pulling the fumes inside. All around the road, the land seemed to be closing down around us, the trees leaning in like a tunnel of old bones.

I talked him up to a wrecked ridgeback the old sawmillers used to call Tickle Cut. It was high and clear of the burn area. I had him pull over.

"Why stop, Daddy? There ain't nothing to see."

Even as he asked it, he slowed and eased up onto a solid bank. He cut the engine and we both got out.

We could see the whole drunken spread of fire coming on through the valley, a bright thread of flames and the bundle of smoke like long gray hair in the wind. It was eating everything up, coming on to the cove where Daddy's cabin sat. We were too far away to hear anything, but

Godamighty it was burning now, tearing the mountains apart. The hell that men had put there was running a true course, and there was nothing in the world to stop it. I stared at the burn, wondering how a man could put a spark on all that, how we had let it happen. I don't know exactly why I kept watching, why I didn't let Tommy take me on home. But I wanted to drive the pain of it through my eyes and into my brain. Bury it there like a hot needle.

Crystal Wilkinson

Fixing Things

an excerpt from *The Birds of Opulence*

The house feels three-legged to Joe now that Lucy's gone. In her last days she was smoking up a storm and seeing ghosts with that scared, sad look on her face. Though he had always thought there was nothing he couldn't fix, Joe had been helpless against those things that twisted Lucy's mind. He could fix a car, fix a broken gasket, an axe handle, anything with a motor. Folks always asking him to fix this and that. But he'd been helpless to fix much aside from those mechanical things all the years he had lived with these Goode women. Since he'd married Lucy all those years ago.

At five in the morning, he goes out to his pickup. The dew is still fresh on the windshield and an early morning spider web catches him in the face. He places three potted plants on the passenger's seat and places a hoe and a metal bucket in the truck bed.

It's the day after Lucy's funeral. The sky is brightening up but the sun still shows itself as a muted red ball on the horizon. The trees on the knob are black silhouettes, as though the heat of the sun has charred them.

With everything quiet, Joe fights the urge to turn on the radio, and he doesn't. When he crosses the bridge and heads out into the country, he hears dogs barking from backyards. He's never owned a dog, never let his children have one. Didn't think it was right to have them chained to a stake out back.

As the sun rises, everything that had looked dead changes into shades of green and brown. He drives as slow as the tourists who are starting to swarm downtown. Most of them are crowding into The

Depot Restaurant. It used to be the old Greyhound bus station but now has the long-front-porch feel of a Cracker Barrel and has a tin roof and huge wooden boxes of bright red geraniums. The tourists cram inside it to look at the trinkets, mostly cheap replicas of things found over at the Opulence Museum. They flock to the postcards, the stationery and old-fashioned toys—spinning tops and real wooden checkers and metal jacks and such—but they come back for Callie Sumner's collards and her fried chicken, and the Formica kitchen tables covered in gingham tablecloths, old-fashioned salt and pepper shakers, and Mason jars of sweet iced tea. This kind of foolishness, trying to grab so tightly onto something that used to be, makes Joe laugh, but mostly he wishes these tourists would find somewhere else to go. He has become skeptical of city folks though he had once been one himself, before he moved here looking for work when he was twenty. It's hard for him to believe that he was ever one of those young city men with a bit of a swagger who made fun of anyone with a country accent. Now, though he remembers his silver-tongued beginnings, he belongs fully to Opulence and the people here. He is more a Goode than a Brown. He is sure of that now.

The farmers, who'd most likely been up before daylight, throw their hands up at him and he nods back. He notices that there are not as many black farmers out here as there used to be. Most of them either passed away or left the country for work in the city years ago. And not many of the children ever came back after they moved off to college. He sees the farmers along the way on tractors, with hoes or rakes in their hands. The dairy farmers with their buckets. Otis Turner cleaning out a pig stall. All that work being done makes him think about all the weed eaters and lawnmowers in his shed that need fixing. Mrs. MacAfee has asked him to come by and look at her dishwasher and he has a chisel plow in the driveway that a man from Bracktown wants him to look at.

When he reaches the entrance of the home place it is covered with weeds. He knows the Goode place is owned by someone else, city white folks he figures, but no matter. This isn't the first time he's been out here since the sale. Every so often he comes here just to sit in his truck and think. Sometimes he takes pleasure in watching the birds perched in the trees feeding their young.

Once, he brought Lucy with him hoping that the fresh air would do her some good. She sat right down in the garden and got eaten up by the chiggers. Seemed she had divorced herself from this land long ago, back when Yolanda was born out here in the squash patch. He remembers that night she refused to nurse the baby and how the smell of women's blood and sour milk had taken up the entire room. He remembers the rain ping-pinging on the window, how much he loved Lucy. He could have never left her side no matter how crazy she was. Least folks thought she was crazy. He's not sure even now. Could have been some kind of sign from God for all he knows. He remembers that after she calmed down and the women forced her to feed the baby how quiet everything was, how even with the cloudy night he could see the outline of the trees out the window. Remembers how much he loved her then and how he's loved her all these years since.

It seems to him that the new owners have abandoned the Goode place. No sign that the grounds have been maintained. Miss Minnie Mae had prided herself in keeping it cut and kempt. She had hired a couple of the farmers down the road to bush-hog it at the turn of spring and then keep it mowed all summer.

Though it is falling down even more now, he can still see the chimney of the old house; the rotting lumber where the well used to be; the overturned smokehouse. He could easily walk it with his eyes closed now after all these years. He knows it foot by foot. He wishes he had come up with the money June and Butter asked for when they sold it to the white man.

He removes the pots from the truck and sits them on the ground. Then takes the hoe and the water bucket from the truck bed.

He's got some age on him but his stride is good. He carries the first pot out to a spot just beyond the well, facing the hills. The morning is brisk and he feels the chill across his cheeks.

He takes up the hoe and digs, plants the first flower, and as he pours the water he closes his eyes and says, "Minnie Mae Goode, wife of Henry Goode. A fine woman, an old-time woman. Amen."

He plants the second bush where he thinks the daffodils used to grow up near the house. "Nora Jean Goode, Tookie they called her. Woman had a hard life, but she loved us every one. Amen."

He then goes to the garden spot, which is easy to find, because the onions have grown wild and are sprouting all over. He can't help but to marvel, like he does every time he comes here, that his daughter was born in this garden even in modern times. He digs the hole, plants the rosebush and says, "For my beloved Lucy. Mother of my children. My life. Amen." His voice box chokes up and the words don't come out as strong as he intended. "Amen, Amen, Amen," he says and then stands back and looks at the good work he's done.

He stands looking around the place thinking about Lucy's last days and how she kept on talking about ghosts. She'd been going on about her mother, her grandmother, her great grandmother. "Lucy, them old women did the best they could," he'd told her. Kitchen ghosts, she'd called them. Kept saying, "Mama gone. Granny gone. Roots still here." For the life of him he still doesn't know what she meant. Must've been her mind talking. Them pills didn't do any good.

And then Yolanda with those spells, those panic attacks as she calls them. He wonders if he might have brought this on his family somehow. He can't help but think if he'd tried hard enough he could have fixed it—like a sputtering engine or a battery gone bad. He hangs his head and looks at the grass. The flowers are beginning to bud, their little heads straining toward the light and away from the soil. He could stay here a week and no one would find him. *But the children would worry.* He thinks of Yolanda and Kee Kee riding along the back roads in search of him, grieving again. He can't bear the thought of them losing someone else. He is all they have now. He puts his hands in his pocket and kicks at a beetle. He wonders if there are any copperheads thawing out and ready to strike.

Behind him he hears an engine and of course he knows it's a Mack truck before he turns around. If he listens closely, Joe is sure he could identify the exact style. He turns around and a man with a ruddy face and a red flannel shirt steps from the cab. He is unshaven and Joe notices his lips are chapped as though he is a man in need of water.

"You got reason to be here?"

"This was my family's land. Just paying respects to our kin that's crossed over. That's all."

The man says, "Well get it done because we are about to build a pond out here."

Joe realizes that the Goodes were never his biological family, but he'd found his place among them and would fight to the death for any Goode alive, except for maybe Butter and June.

"Ain't never been no pond here," Joe says. "Used to be a. . . ."

"Old man, you best get going." The man wipes sweat from his forehead and looks at his watch.

Joe sees a hummingbird on the honeysuckle along the fence row and stands there watching it. He closes his eyes against finding Lucy on the kitchen floor bled out from her wrist and how there was nothing he could do to fix it. Nothing no doctor could do either. When he had tried to sleep last night, that image kept popping into his head and he woke up in a cold sweat. He missed her beside him.

"I'm going," Joe says.

He walks slowly toward his pickup.

"Get on with it then. We've got a day's work at least."

The truck revs up and heads for the center of the property and two men roll off a Caterpillar. Joe stands and watches the men doing their work. He kneels down in the dirt, whispers every Goode name he has ever heard spoken and pours the remaining water in the bucket onto the ground.

He thinks of Lucy when they first married and how her mother and grandmother had told stories up into the night before he and Lucy took to their marriage bed. His initiation, he thinks now. He remembers how wide they opened their arms to him and how quickly they took him for their own. He shifts the weight of his hips to try and keep his right knee from flaring up again. Lately he has been plagued by bursitis.

He knows he should get in his pickup and move on back toward home, but he stays there watching as they dig down into the dirt to make way for this pond. He's sure the children are back at the house by now wondering where he is. The women have made casseroles and pies and are standing on the porch waiting to soothe him in his mourning time. His friends have gathered with their pints. They will wait for the women to leave before they get down to men's business. He knows there will be gossip about the way Lucy crossed over, but he is past the age to care about all of that.

He stands there, invisible to the working men. Stands while the hole in the earth widens, and sees the land devoured by the machine and the shovels. He is sure that if he lays his head on the ground he will hear the voices of the Goode clan bringing in the day with a dirge.

When he leaves the home place it is well past noon. He rides back toward his house convinced that all that's left there are those things out back that need fixing. After the children and the grandchildren and the church women and his friends have left, he will be alone for the second night in more years than he can remember.

A week from now, though he will still be filled with a deep sadness, Joe will roar with laughter.

John Turner, one of the farmers, will walk into the little store where the workers come to jabber and whittle.

"Joe," he'll say. "Did you hear what happened?"

Every man in the store will stop and want to hear the story. They'll hover over their hog's head cheese and bologna sandwiches wrapped in white butcher paper. They'll stop gulping down their little Coca-Colas filled with peanuts to listen.

"Hoot told me that them men that bought up Miss Minnie's place was just a-digging on that pond. They dug and dug all week but wasn't quite finished so they left their bulldozer parked up on the side there. Up by that bank."

All the men will shake their heads. They will all know just the spot.

"Right up there. You know where that little hill next to the smokehouse dips down a little?"

"Yeah," Joe will say.

"Well if it don't beat the devil, but them old boys left that Caterpillar in that spot where some of them old-time people had found that underground spring years ago."

The men will nod knowingly in unison.

"They say this old man had witched that well there. But anyway, on Saturday it come the awfulest rain you ever did see. . . ."

The men will lean in close because Turner's always been a fine story-teller. They'll be quiet as children restless for the end. Turner'll stop and chuckle a bit and make them wait for what comes next.

"When them old boys come back on Monday all they could see is the tip-top of the seat of that dozer. Said the man that bought the place had to pay double to have somebody come out there and pull that dozer out before they could start up again. We all been laughing about it out yonder since."

Turner will slap his thigh then slap Joe on the back.

"Miss Minnie's people done come back and gave them folks a piece of their minds. I wouldn't be a bit surprised if it wuddn't Miss Minnie herself leading them all to flood that dozer out."

All the men will laugh, but it will be Joe Brown who will laugh the loudest and the longest because deep down he will know it to be true.

Jake Adam York

Letter to Be Wrapped Around a Bottle of Whiskey

for Bob Morgan

Water so thick
light just stumbles through
the cordials you've poured,
making a welcome table
of the cedar chest
the glasses lens
in some compound eye
to observe the story
of a rug or a plank
or a glass of whiskey.
Body and plant, body
and land, conversations
are naturalists
or rivers, knowing
the schist and the batholith,
ginseng and Genesis,
gathering as they go.
Rise into the balds,
following streams
to their first ideas,
and the fork of the voice
will tremble, strike rock,
and draw the flood.
As corn, once wheat-thin,
will rise from any ground.

As it holds its sugars,
days it's concentrated
to such brightness
we distill, thought
to form, in the hollows
where we remembered
how to cut cadence
from a limb, a ballad
from a family
tree. As the maker of fire
brings the guitar
and the country song
from a turtle's shell
and the stomach of a lamb.
As what begins anywhere
started already somewhere
else. Here, in the ridge
and valley of voice
where you draw the well of song,
the spring that's warming now
in your talk, maybe
it is snowing now,
and a string band threads
the bruise of night
where windows are
crocuses offering their saffrons
to the cold and the snake-handler's
arms in the one-room church
antennas raised
to the broadcast Christ,
the zircon in his pocket
shaking the mustard seed
from the mockingbird,
gospel from the air,
the peavine of melody curling

on his tongue an air
the wanderers know,
having passed mouth
to mouth, over the sea,
guitar to glossolalia
in tangled lines.
As from the stalk
the pone and the potable,
from the blue-hole
the bluegrass and the blues,
you keep pouring,
so conversations are naturalists
and rivers, each step,
each stumble an address
to the ground or the stars,
until we are chests,
until we are rooms,
until we are radios
playing all stations,
a ballad on every one.

Walt Whitman in Alabama

Maybe on his way to Gadsden,
Queen City of the Coosa,
to speak with the pilots and inland sailors,
to cross the fords Jackson ran with blood
or meet the mayor who
bought the ladies' favors with river quartz,
maybe east from some trip west to see
or returning north from New Orleans
or just lost in those years after The War

as legend has it, after the bannings,
when he'd grown tired of puffs and plates,
after he'd grown the beard and begun
to catch things there he had to walk off
or sing unwritten, maybe when the open road
opened on mockingbirds two and two—
no one knows, though the stories have him here
recapturing Attalla, shaking poems from his hair
on the steps of local churches. Maybe
it was the end of many letters, the last
of hospital days, another sleight
to make his hand come alive
when he couldn't bring some Southron home.
I see him there remembering his poems,
his back to the door, singing
out to the garden of the world,
the tropical spring of pine and jasmine,
how wondrous it was the pent-up river
washed to green their farms, the creeks swole
with mountain dew to sprout the corn,
herbage of poke and collard,
spinach and bean, to wash the roots
of every leaf to come. But more
I wonder what he did not say,
whether the doors were closed on the room
where none thought Jesus ever naked,
whether he went down Gadsden's Broad
to the bluff where a hundred years thence
someone fabled a child lost from the arms
of his Hispanic mother and almost saved
by a cop who brought from his pocket
a shirt's worth of proof before the woman
vanished with her English, before the psychics
started rowing down the channel
to listen for the baby's dreams—all years after

the whorehouses, the fires, Reconstruction
and true religion came, after Whitman said his piece
and left the county to its mayors,
its wars and local dramas, Broad Street
and its theatres to opening and closing
and being torn down to photograph and rumor
where Vaudeville variety traveled
in those years before the world became real
and history stilled, before the dams stalled
the yearly flood that washed the roots
and made new fields from catfish and shit
and the mountain dead, before
the sun in the tassels was wormed to shine,
before shine dried into the hills
with the snakes, the poetry, the legend.
I imagine him here in the different city,
bathing in the yellow light as the river slips
beneath the bridge, flickering like a candle
or like the body or like the bodies
lit up with gasoline and beer, tremble of taillights,
while the statue of the Civil War heroine
points fingerless down Broad, down the stream
of headlamps and embers of burning weed,
a congregation in which his secrets and his song
would be unwelcome, though he slake
some secret thirsts, his orotund voice
tune our ears to the river's whisper,
a baby cradled in branches
deep beneath the bridge.
Its ribs filter the Coosa's brown.
Its arms raise the crops.
And every night it whispers the town
in some new forgotten tongue.

Knoxville Girl

(Traditional) Arranged by Charlie and Ira Louvin. Recorded May 3, 1956.

The song is one their mother sang,
a campfire waltz on autumn nights
or alone, a lullaby,
the oldest song they know.

Now the tape is rolling,
Charlie on guitar, Ira mandolin,
the way they've done since they were kids,
in heirloom melody—

*I met a little girl in Knoxville,
a town we all know well—*
their voices twine, almost one,
the harmony almost gospel.

But this is not a hymn.
They walk the riverside, whittling
smooth that driftwood branch
they'll use to *strike that fair girl down*

where she'll plead for mercy, life,
dark eyes twinkling
like the river in the wind
as they *only beat her more.*

They'll grab her *by her golden curls*
and *drag her round and round,*
and *throw her into the river*
that runs through Knoxville town.

•

In the song, they never pause,
but run on home to bed and dream
her singing hush-now rhymes
while the sheriff fiddles at the door,

and we never see her raised
from the stream's thick water.
But the song is old,
and she has waited years before

in the Thames and the Tennessee
for her miller, her minstrel, her country boy
to call her back, then strike her down
and lay her in the stream,

her hair a wild anemone,
a millweed that snakes like flame
to light the sheriff's page,
an ancient tongue in guilty mouths,

or moonlight through the bars
of the cinder-block *cell*
where they sit for *killing that Knoxville girl,*
that girl they *loved so well.*

Sweat gleams on the guitar's face.
Ira holds the chord in the mandolin
till the wood is still.
They wait as the tape rolls out,

smoothing like a stream to hold
sky's last light,
till she's still and quiet
as a lullaby child.

ARTIST STATEMENTS

NIN ANDREWS

William Faulkner stayed on our farm when I was a baby. How's that for name-dropping? Just saying the name, William Faulkner, is my way of saying the name of God. I never say it in vain. My father always said you have to have something to say when you're dying, and I do. William Faulkner, I will say, thank you. I am not certain if Faulkner stayed on our farm for a night, a month, or the whole year he was teaching at UVA, but my father made it sound as if he moved right in and never left again. Just like everyone else on the farm. Folks walked up our dirt road, sometimes not even wearing shoes, and they stuck around. *Just like stray cats*, my mother commented. Like Toby who caught snapping turtles in our pond and carried them on his back in a burlap sack. He said he caught them by feeling in the mud with his toes. Like Mary who came by Yellow Cab carrying a little red suitcase and moved right into the house to help raise *the chillens*, as she called us. Like Mr. Shaver who had only one arm and said one was good enough for tossing horseshoes, shooting groundhogs, and working the land. Like Timmy who shot his wife and worked on the farm before and after he went to prison. As my father put it, *a good farm-hand is hard to find*. Thinking of my parents' dark humor and the voices from the past, I feel a kind of homesickness I carry with me like an ache in my bones. Their voices inform my poems of the South.

Of course, if you're anything like me, all you really want to hear about is Faulkner. The truth is, I was a newborn then, or I was about to be born. I don't know which. But my parents told stories. Lots of them. In one story they said he drank a lot and didn't talk much. But he loved to go horseback riding alone. Late afternoons, he would saunter down to the barn and ask if he could take one of our mares out for a trail ride by himself. He always chose the same feisty mare, and that mare always bucked him off. My father tried to talk him into taking another horse. *William,* my father asked, *Why don't you try Sugar Lump instead? Sugar Lump will give you a nice easy ride. A sack of potatoes could stay on her back all day long.* But William Faulkner must not have liked being compared to a sack of potatoes. At the end of the day, he would be seen walking across the pasture, his riding cap in his hand, the shadows growing tall behind him. *A writer always does want the horse who pitches him off,* he said. Years later I wondered if that was a better description of a writer, or just any man.

MAKALANI BANDELE

My daddy's family is from Needmore, Kentucky, which is a little Black community outside of Danville. My momma is from Springfield, Kentucky, specifically Briartown, the small black community on the outskirts. I come from liars (storytellers), musicians, and dancers. My maternal grandfather was a very good banjo player; he played for White and Black folks' dances and occasions. Consequently, my momma and her sisters could cut a rug like nobody's business. My daddy's people weren't especially musical to my knowledge, and they could dance, but they primarily like to have a good time and tell lies. So, from a young age I was bathed in the twin African-American traditions of orality and music. Thus, my interest in putting words together in creative ways comes from my fascination with and desire to participate in the storytelling and repartee I heard going on in my family, and really whenever I was around Black people. My poetics are largely made up of an experiment to capture and contain the nuances of an African-American worldview, as well as the arts of African-American speech and music within a wild, poetic line. I am concerned with how to write poems that are as imaginative and musical, that is to say funky, as they can be. This translates into poems rhythmically or sonically interesting, but also funky in how ideas or a collage of images might excite the reader's imagination to dance.

BRIAN BARKER

When the Bower brothers returned from hunting, their old barge of a car creaked down the road, rust-pocked and listing dangerously over the center line, then swerving into the steep, rutted gravel drive where it bounced on worn-out shocks, grinding to an abrupt halt. The boys, six or seven of them—all lanky and over six feet tall, with self-inflicted bowl haircuts—unfolded themselves from the backseat like a troupe of contortionists. Then somebody unlatched the trunk and a pack of bird dogs bounded out, gasping for air, tongues lolling, shaking their heads and sneezing in the sunlight. How many dogs were there? Six? Seven? One for each brother? Gorgeous, perfect creatures, they seemed to keep coming, as if the trunk had a false bottom. Sleek and spotted, all ears and legs, they bayed and nipped and crashed into one another, loping around the rusted-out detritus that dotted the yard.

This collision of the beautiful and the brutal embodies my Appalachia. It's a contradiction deeply engrained in the landscape and the people— one of abundance and poverty, kindness and violence, piousness and sin. It's a complicated place that cannot be easily summed up, no matter how hard outsiders try. I write from the crux of this contradiction, jimmying open the trunk of some jalopy and bracing myself for whatever beautiful thing might come bounding from the dark, knocking me down into a cloud of dust, then standing over me, hot and slobbering, its soft jowls speckled with blood.

PINCKNEY BENEDICT

When I was a boy, my old man—who was like a king in our house and on our farm generally—always insisted that there were only two kinds of people in the world: mountain people and flatlanders. His pronunciation of the word *flatlanders* was full of freezing contempt. The unspoken war between these radically opposed populations, I came to understand, was akin to the war between Heaven and Hell: all but eternal, hopeless in appearance, but eventually—after eons of bloody struggle—to be won by the forces of light. "Orgo" is my effort, all these years later, to work out on paper that boyhood understanding of the true nature of the world.

PAULA BOHINCE

My Appalachia is represented by a kind of shabby beauty, a beauty *in spite of,* through images of woods and fields, creatures and property, faith and poverty. I see a buck poised in woods with a weakling sun anointing his antlers; feeding does near him, the bent arrows of their necks pointing to earth; a fawn, new and trembling, in dead leaves. I see then the broken neck of one of them along the roadside and the pickup trucks that amble by. I see the hung adult: shot, bleeding upside down before the butchering. My Pennsylvania is felt through an unromantic immersion in nature, with a soft wonder among the decline and nostalgia.

With "Cleaning My Father's House," the homestead that was in my family for three generations—from the ancestors' arrival from Slovenia, through decades of work in the coal mines, until my father's death—is emptied. But what becomes of that accumulation? "Heaven" reflects my wish for persistence and safety, in the midst of change, in a house sliding off a strip-mined mountain. What is the future of this land? What hand or net waits for a place that "wants to be caught"? In "The Children," the chasm between generations is immense, and negotiations between are a kind of time travel and renewal, as the cornfield transforms into a site for drugs and sex and music.

JOHN E. BRANSCUM

Human. A thing you can forget. Like childhood. Like a baby in a hot car. Especially in the toad shadows of the mountains, away from the lights of other houses, other hearts, way up high, in rarefied air, in poverty, in despair, a living demanding a breathing other than (Less than? More than? In addition to? In subtraction from?) human—like the way liquor makes you breathe, or sex, or the gods.

For my daddy's people, due to blood or curse, as soon as we walked out of the house, such a forgetting would occur. We'd disappear into hunting or fishing, into the jacked-up speed of $500 Chevy Novas, into men and women, into gangs, into woods. We'd learned semipermeability, learned how much we belonged to the land and everything that lived upon it, learned that if you stare long enough at something it gets inside you. In other words, as a people and a culture, we're prone to changing into things—some of them dark. That's the true. Prone to changing from men and women into quarter-timed phone calls. Into crazy stories about crazy doings. Into ghetto window and holler shed. We've spent too long staring at the dirt, you see—at the broken glass, at the night sky, at the trees, staring at the falling stars with our hands inside kills and imagined revenges. And so our skins have become other skins. Bear skins. Deer skins. Wolf skins. Fancy suits. Timberlands. Nikes. The skins of our fathers. Of our mothers. Of the mountains. These skins have leaked through to our souls. They leak out when we write.

DENNIS COVINGTON

We Covingtons were lanky, slope-shouldered, and sharp-chinned. We had a dark sense of humor, a mania for solitude. We were quick to get our backs up. But we were also prone to sentimentality. At the drop of a hat, we'd confess everything we'd ever done. We'd tell more than anybody wanted to hear. So when they turned a deaf ear, we'd sing it to them, or bang it out on the piano or guitar. We were undignified, but honest. We prayed, worked hard, and knew there'd be a place for us in the great by and by. But I didn't really know where we'd come from until I met the snake-handlers of Southern Appalachia. When I sat down to write about them, a voice poured out of me that I'd never heard before. It was dissonant and harsh, plaintive but melodic, and I realized it was the voice of my people, a gift from the generation of Covingtons who'd come down from the mountains. I knew that voice was the only power I'd ever have, and the only inheritance worth fighting for.

JEFF MANN

I'm a Southerner, an Appalachian, and a gay man. That complex set of identities guarantees conflict both inner and outer, but such conflict only provides fodder for my creativity. Everything I write—poetry, fiction, and literary nonfiction—is pervaded by those selves and those struggles. Gay desire, homomasculinity, my Celtic and Teutonic bloodlines, the Appalachian landscape I revere, the mountain-folk culture I relish, the repressive and fundamentalist religions I detest, and the fevered and painful history of the American South, a legacy I feel more and more deeply with each passing year: these things have made me the man and the writer that I am. They have nurtured my appreciation of the erotic, my awareness of the tragic, my gratitude for the comic, and have convinced me of the value of ornery persistence and defiant endurance.

MAURICE MANNING

Writing poems is a way to continue learning and to keep thinking. It leads to new things and connects them with old things. Poetry is also a particular method of thought; it rambles around and sees what it can see, and it comes up to something stark and bracing suddenly. When I want to learn this way Kentucky is the book I open first. It is the one I grew up with and the one I have loved my whole life. My people and their times are recorded here and the place itself is a voice telling me a story. It is humbling to be the listener.

DESIRAE MATHERLY

Southern Appalachia was always a place I tried to escape from. It wasn't until I became an academic and an expatriate that I developed homesickness. Mostly I missed the feel of familiar words in my mouth, their gravity and naturalness. When writing, I continue the old masquerade, though I live in the present of East Tennessee, of pickup trucks, biscuits and brown gravy, mountain hikes, and bluegrass pickers at the farmers' market on Saturdays. From my deep memory, old men chewing tobacco at the service station where we returned our glass bottles for deposit, and brown skin in jean cutoffs swimming at the lake, before the rich Northerners bought up the shoreline. An adolescence spent topping, cutting, hanging, and grading tobacco, or loading hay into the barn; walking barefoot through the garden and riding my horse without a saddle in the moonlight. This too—of drunken fights between my stepfather and mother in a trailer with a rotten bathroom floor and olive shag carpeting; of camping and camo tarps, sauceburgers in aluminum foil; Sundays at the Baptist church with my grandmother's strong alto and several others mostly out of tune and drawling. Of swearing that I'd leave and never come back. (*Never*.) Of coming back, and finding some of those things gone, and realizing that there's no such thing as leaving. And now, the shock of seeing Appalachia's bizarre contrary qualities like tiny vestigial limbs in my essays, as if I could ever be someone else, from any other world.

DAVIS MCCOMBS

It's a stretch to say that I'm "Appalachian" in any way (more Ozarkan these days than anything else), but it is true that I keep writing myself back to an area of Kentucky where I haven't lived in nearly a decade. Poems that start out elsewhere have a tendency, through the twists of revision, to find their way back to the caves and Caveland of Hart, Barren, and Edmonson counties where I grew up.

KAREN SALYER MCELMURRAY

Some nights when I can't sleep, what I remember is a building. A place called the warm house, where canned goods and potatoes and beets were stored for the winter. Was that building in Dwale or Waylon or Hagerhill? Or in some other memory-town I sometimes need so badly I can taste it? It is those towns and buildings, the green glass of canning jars and the smooth skins of beets that I try to summon when I write about my home place in Eastern Kentucky. Much of that home is long gone, these days. One house was taken when a public highway went through. Aunts and uncles, grandmothers and grandfathers. Many have passed on. But I'm lucky, I guess. Some people are losing whole mountaintops these days. I'm lucky, how clearly I remember standing in that warm house, beside an opening into a stone floor. Spring water fed up into the building to keep it cool. The shiny, black water, if you stood and stared down into it in the dark, was smooth and still, almost peaceful.

SARA PRITCHARD

I like to sleep with my hand on the wall. The wall is hard, substantial, textured, cool. My hand's a stethoscope, and I can feel the rush and thump of the world beyond, hear the deer tiptoeing through the cemetery, the ants chomping away on the peonies, the stars settling in, the little gray catbird crying in the yews, the rustle of light, the mourning dove's *coo-coo*, the wheeling of wings. I have to sleep with a heating pad on my gimp hip, so there's this eternal convection going on from the radiance and *energeia* of this world, through cool plaster and fire in the bones, and back out into the wholly holy all.

ALLY REEVES

"Origins" is a brief excerpt from "Appalachia Out," Book 1 in the three-book series *Southern Fried Masala*. Images in the writing flow from a variety of sources, many being photos from my family history and childhood; others, xeroxed photos of Appalachian crazy quilts, Gujarati textiles, and religious paintings from India's past. Weaving the biographies of a handful of women into one conglomerate "biography," *Southern Fried Masala* charts the course of a character who offers a disjointed recollection of her life and attempts to fulfill a personal vow of self-determination.

"Origins" begins in the foggy mountains of Appalachia where we discover our character's roots—we're not sure. Clealand is a moody character whose "I" becomes "We" without warning, and whose body is both human and animal. It is Clealand's childhood dream of limitless possibility and "a sense of wonder" that acts as both a lantern in the darkness and a raging fire that threatens to burn down all the character has built.

Southern Fried Masala examines the delicate balance between creativity and destruction, brilliance and ignorance, fame and infamy. Through the lives of women who eat soil, take antidepressants, and gather themselves for what will be a historical flight, we discover unbearable moments of beauty and the glory of being just "OK."

R. T. SMITH

Improvisation. To my way of thinking, that's the most undeniable ingredient in the Appalachian profile, perhaps because it's the most necessary. Make-shift, jury-rigged, winging it, making do. The irregularities of topography and weather, interventions, water and blood and spirits. While custom and convention play strong roles in the lives of farmers, believers, musicians, storytellers, millers and weavers and healers, the need to adapt and revise is ubiquitous. No surprise Sarah Carter would find a new way of playing mountain music, just as Dock and Doc, Earl, Edden, Jimmie, and a host of others would.

As a species, we resemble magpies, constructing our nests and rituals with the available and imaginable, but almost inevitably an Appalachian magpie's medley will not be a jumble or a muddle so much as an artful accommodation constructed in part from family practices, religious influences, a yearning for precision and rebellion, a nod to flora and fauna and rock formations, currents and echoes, passion and rationale, mischief and awareness of death. "Work for the night is coming," says the hymn, and Appalachians feel it in every breath but measure their lives to fetch delight where hardship and darkness pervade and test every step.

BIANCA SPRIGGS

Much of my work has been called "what-if" poetry. I grew up reading a spectrum of fictive works, from folktales and ancient myths to science-fiction, fantasy, and genre-fiction, work that propelled my imagination out of a home often fraught with friction. From an early age, these alternate worlds provided a way for me to navigate concepts that I didn't understand. My training began very early as someone who is comfortable dwelling in the terra incognita of magical realism, or negotiating the common ground between ordinary and speculative events in an attempt to reveal a third space, wherein the patterns and motives that guide humanity and the natural world dwell. And because I consider myself a Southern writer, one connected directly to Appalachia, I identify with issues that pertain primarily to my region through my writing. Thanks to my Affrilachian Poet family, I have been reared in the literary tradition of putting the land and its people first. For me, this region occupies not just its distinctive geographical space, but also a uniquely American cultural space.

ALEX TAYLOR

I was born and raised in the Western Coal Fields region of Kentucky. We have hills and hollers but no mountains. My accent is different from the folks who live in the eastern part of the state, more drawl than twang. This being said, I believe it holds true that Appalachia and Western Kentucky aren't totally dissimilar. Both are impoverished regions where mysticism and religiosity are still palpable forces. I hope "A Lakeside Penitence" communicates to some degree the healthy presence of myth in Kentucky. Places, as well as people, are haunted in my state and I liken the storyteller's charge to that of the conjurer, an artist who inhabits the two realms of existence—the spiritual and the physical—and who must, at all times, be willing to live in the liminal space between.

JACINDA TOWNSEND

I wrote *Saint Monkey* as a love letter to a Black Appalachian culture that has all but disappeared. On the perimeter of Lexington, newly freed slaves founded small villages such as Maddoxtown, New Zion, and Fort Spring and went to work on the area's farms. Kentucky's horse-breeding history is full of Black folk: fourteen of the fifteen jockeys in the first Kentucky Derby were Black. Today, these hamlets—and this history—have almost been erased. The vibrant Black culture that remains is informed by the mores of our antecedents, but the last people who remember tapping their feet in time to slave spirituals just before the church processional are now septuagenarians, and I wanted to write a snapshot of a place in time and earth that is being buried before it can even be recorded. "Lackland" is a piece that grew out of a story my father told me about his months at Lackland Air Force Base. The basics of it are biographical: as my father told me, he rarely set foot off base because of the viciousness of Jim Crow in the Deep South. Oddly enough, Kentucky—the Whitest state south of Vermont—had been, on balance, much kinder to him.

JESSIE VAN EERDEN

As the landscape of my imagination, Appalachia always informs my work—the mountains' humidity, rhythms of speech, creek names. But, to phrase it a little differently, Appalachia is also the landscape of my soul, such that the region's power to shape my writing lies not so much in its trilliums coming up along Wilson Hill, which climbs to my childhood home, or in its silvery bark exposed in winter (an image that lived in my head during my years deep in the evergreens of the Northwest)— its power lies in the way Appalachia taught me to meet people, people who spoke of the soul without embarrassment, a dense web of people, many of whom populate "Woman with Spirits." I am still learning how to meet people, and Appalachia, I think, is still teaching me. In *I and Thou*, Martin Buber claims that we need to have our individual beings confirmed by our "genuine meetings," but, beyond this, we need "to see that the truth, which the soul gains by its struggle, is flashing up for the other . . . in a different way, and equally confirmed." True meeting gives a respectful nod to the hard truths earned by the one facing you on the road: this is the kind of meeting valued by the folks I grew up around, valued more highly, perhaps, because of the threat of caricature—idealization and scorn—ever looming. I wrote this piece as a direct address so as to signal this kind of meeting, or my effort toward it.

CHARLES DODD WHITE

"Controlled Burn" was a chance for me to talk about what is an increasing dichotomy in my part of the world: the rise of an immigrant labor class and the decline of Scots-Irish families betrayed by bottom-line capitalistic ethics. These two forces, like many similar historical conflicts, eat away at the decency and respect people in better days have for one another. I saw a chance to portray this ongoing conflict against another small but dangerous segment, the antigovernment isolationist, who introduces apocalyptic fear into a society in the midst of profound change. The resulting action of the fire and the absurdity of "controlling" any action or entity so inherently chaotic testifies to my belief that these movements are much larger and historic than we can currently understand.

JAKE ADAM YORK

I grew up in the toes of the Appalachians, not far from the Southern terminus of Lookout Mountain. Until I was thirteen, I spent every morning in my grandmother's kitchen, eating the farmer's breakfast—eggs, bacon, ham, sausage, grits, toast, and jam—while she made the day's cornpone. Her AM radio was on beside the stove, giving us WAAX's mixture of classic country and Paul Harvey while she told another story about growing up on the farm, her father's store, her mother snapping the heads off snakes, or the shadowy great-great-grandmother who, supposedly, walked out of the Cherokee towns of East Tennessee or North Carolina, ready to buy every little White girl an ice cream cone except her own, whom she sent to the cotton mill every day, whose week's wage—a dime—always went elsewhere. When the pone was done, it came out of the oven, was flipped, fell from the skillet in a single gesture, crusted dark as a meteor, according to a recipe (cornmeal, buttermilk, a pinch of flour, baking powder (no eggs!)) I later found in a Cherokee cookbook. At dinner, she and my grandfather would pass the honeydew and recite the list of melons they used to eat, but which are gone because the seedfreezers all died. These are the seeds they gave me. I keep them dry and ready for the ground.

CONTRIBUTORS

Nin Andrews is the editor of a book of translations of the French poet Henri Michaux entitled *Someone Wants to Steal My Name* (Cleveland State University Press). She is also the author of several books, including *The Book of Orgasms, Why They Grow Wings, Midlife Crisis with Dick and Jane, Dear Professor, Do You Live in a Vacuum, Sleeping with Houdini,* and *The Secret Life of Mannequins.* Her collection *Southern Comfort* was published by CavanKerry Press.

Makalani Bandele is an Affrilachian Poet and Louisville, Kentucky, native. He is the recipient of the Ernest Sandeen Poetry Award and a fellowship from Cave Canem Foundation. His poems can be read in various online and print journals. *Hellfightin',* published by Willow Books in October 2011, is his first full-length volume of poetry.

Brian Barker is the author of *The Animal Gospels* (Tupelo Press, 2006) and *The Black Ocean* (Southern Illinois University Press, 2011), winner of the Crab Orchard Open Competition. He teaches at the University of Colorado Denver where he coedits *Copper Nickel.*

Pinckney Benedict grew up in rural West Virginia. He has published four books of fiction, most recently *Miracle Boy and Other Stories.* His work has been published in *Esquire, Zoetrope, O. Henry Prize Stories, The Pushcart Prize, Best New Stories from the South,* and *The Oxford Book of the American Short Story.*

Paula Bohince is the author of *The Children* (2012) and *Incident at the Edge of Bayonet Woods* (2008), both from Sarabande. She has served as the Amy Lowell Poetry Travelling Scholar and the Dartmouth Poet in Residence at the Frost Place. She lives in Pennsylvania.

Dennis Covington is the author of five books, including the memoir *Salvation on Sand Mountain*, a finalist for the National Book Award. His current project involves a search for "the substance of things hoped for" in what some commentators describe as a post-Christian world.

Jeff Mann has published three poetry chapbooks, three full-length books of poetry, two collections of personal essays, a volume of memoir and poetry, two novellas, two novels, and a collection of short fiction. He teaches creative writing at Virginia Tech in Blacksburg, Virginia.

Maurice Manning's *The Common Man* (Houghton Mifflin Harcourt, 2010) was a finalist for the Pulitzer Prize. He teaches at Transylvania University and in the Program for Writers at Warren Wilson College. He lives in Washington County, Kentucky.

Desirae Matherly teaches writing at Tusculum College and serves as nonfiction editor for *The Tusculum Review*. She earned a Ph.D. in creative nonfiction from Ohio University in 2004 and is a former Harper Fellow at the University of Chicago. Recent essays appear in *Hotel Amerika*, *Descant*, and *Painted Bride Quarterly*.

Davis McCombs is the author of *Ultima Thule* (Yale University Press, 2000) and *Dismal Rock* (Tupelo Press, 2007). He is the Director of the Creative Writing Program at the University of Arkansas.

Karen Salyer McElmurray's *Surrendered Child: A Birth Mother's Journey* was an AWP Award Winner for Creative Nonfiction. Her novels are *The Motel of the Stars* and *Strange Birds in the Tree of Heaven*. She currently teaches in the low-residency MFA Programs at West Virginia Wesleyan University and Murray State University.

Donald Ray Pollock was born in 1954 and grew up in southern Ohio, in a holler named Knockemstiff. He dropped out of high school at seventeen to work in a meat-packing plant, and then spent thirty-two years employed in a paper mill in Chillicothe, Ohio. He graduated from the MFA program at Ohio State University in 2009, and still lives in Chillicothe with his wife, Patsy. His first book, *Knockemstiff* (Anchor, 2008), won the 2009 PEN/Robert Bingham Fellowship. *The Devil All the Time* (Anchor), his first novel, was published in 2011.

Sara Pritchard's new story collection, *Help Wanted: Female*, will be published by Etruscan Press in 2013. She lives in West Virginia and teaches fiction in the Wilkes University and the West Virginia Wesleyan low-residency MFA programs.

Ron Rash's most recent book of stories, *Burning Bright*, won the 2010 Frank O'Connor International Short Story Award. He teaches at Western Carolina University.

Ally Reeves currently lives in Mumbai, India, where she works as an artist and designer. Raised in Etowah, Tennessee, a one-stoplight town at the foot of the Smoky Mountains, Reeves' approach to art reflects multifaceted origins: her process and methodology were instilled by an MFA from Carnegie Mellon University and are mingled with the DIY ingenuity born of small towns and nestled anew in India's "maximum city."

R. T. Smith is writer-in-residence at Washington and Lee University, where he serves as editor of *Shenandoah*. His books of poetry include the Library of Virginia Poetry Books of the Year, *Messenger: Poems* (Louisiana State University Press, 2001) and *Outlaw Style: Poems* (University of Arkansas Press, 2007). His fourth book of stories, *Sherburne*, was published in 2012 by Stephen F. Austin Press.

Affrilachian Poet and Cave Canem Fellow **Bianca Spriggs** is a multidisciplinary artist from Lexington, Kentucky. The recipient of a 2013 Al Smith Fellowship, she is the author of *Kaffir Lily* and *How Swallowtails Become Dragons*. In partnership with the Kentucky Domestic Violence

Association, Bianca is the creator of "The SwallowTale Project," a creative writing workshop designed for incarcerated women.

Jane Springer has published two poetry collections, *Dear Blackbird* (University of Utah Press, 2007) and *Murder Ballad* (Alice James Books, 2012), and is the recent recipient of NEA and Whiting fellowships. She currently lives in upstate New York with her husband, son, and two dogs (Woofus and Georgia).

Alex Taylor is originally from Rosine, Kentucky. He is the author of the story collection *The Name of the Nearest River*, published by Sarabande in 2010.

Jacinda Townsend grew up in Bowling Green, Kentucky. A former Fulbright scholar and fiction fellow at the University of Wisconsin, she is the author of the novel *Saint Monkey* (W. W. Norton, 2013). She teaches creative writing at Indiana University and lives in Bloomington with her two children. Visit her website at jacindatownsend.com.

Jessie van Eerden, author of the novel *Glorybound* (WordFarm, 2012), holds an MFA in nonfiction writing from the University of Iowa. Her prose has appeared in *Best American Spiritual Writing, The Oxford American, River Teeth,* and other publications. She lives in West Virginia, where she directs the low-residency MFA program of West Virginia Wesleyan College.

Charles Dodd White lives in western North Carolina. He is author of the story collection *Sinners of Sanction County* and the novel *Lambs of Men*. A recipient of an individual fellowship in prose writing from the North Carolina Arts Council, he is currently at work on his next novel, *Benediction*.

Crystal Wilkinson is the author of *Blackberries, Blackberries* and *Water Street*. Her fiction has been widely published in journals and anthologies. She lives in Lexington, Kentucky, and co-owns The Wild Fig Books.

Jake Adam York was the author of three books of poems—including *A Murmuration of Starlings* (2008) and *Persons Unknown* (2010), published by Southern Illinois University Press in the Crab Orchard Series in Poetry. He was an associate professor at the University of Colorado Denver, where he coedited *Copper Nickel*.

CREDITS

Nin Andrews: "What the Dead See" and "Sundays" from *Southern Comfort* (CavanKerry). Copyright © 2009 by Nin Andrews. "A Brief History of Melvin" first appeared in *Memoir (and)* (Issue 4).

Brian Barker: "In the City of Fallen Rebels" and "Visions for the Last Night on Earth" from *The Black Ocean*. Copyright © 2011 by Brian Barker. Reprinted with the permission of Southern Illinois Press.

Pinckney Benedict: "ORGO vs the FLATLANDERS" printed with permission of the author.

Paula Bohince: "Cleaning My Father's House" and "Heaven" from *Edge of Bayonet Woods* (Sarabande, 2008). "The Children" from *The Children* (Sarabande, 2012).

Dennis Covington: "Desire" first appeared in *Image* (Issue 74, 2012).

Jeff Mann: "715 Willey Street" first appeared in *On the Meaning of Friendship Between Gay Men,* ed. by Andrew Gottlieb (Haworth, 2008) and was reprinted in *Binding the God: Ursine Essays from the Mountain South* by Jeff Mann (Bear Bones Books, 2010).

Maurice Manning: "Culture" first appeared in *Pen America* (Issue 15, 2011). "Provincial Thought" and "The Geography of Yonder" printed with permission of the author.

Desirae Matherly: "Vagina Dentata" originally appeared in *Pleiades: A Journal of New Writing (*29:1).

Davis McCombs: "First Hard Freeze" originally appeared in *Indiana Review* (Summer 2011) and was subsequently published in *Pushcart Prize XXXVII* (W. W. Norton), "Trash Fish" in *Smartish Pace*, and "q & a" in *American Poetry Review*. "Tobacco Culture" from *Dismal Rock* (Tupelo Press, 2007).

Donald Ray Pollock: "Real Life." From *Knockemstiff* by Donald Ray Pollock, copyright © 2008 by Donald Ray Pollock. Used by permission of Doubleday, a division of Random House, Inc. Any third party use of this material, outside of this publication, is prohibited. Interested parties must apply directly to Random House, Inc., for permission.

Sara Pritchard: "The Very Beautiful Sad Elegy for Bambi's Dead Mother" from *Crackpots: A Novel* (Mariner, 2003).

Ron Rash: "Back of Beyond" from *Burning Bright* (Canongate Books, 2011).

R. T. Smith: "The Carter Scratch" from *Outlaw Style: Poems* (University of Arkansas Press, 2007).

Bianca Spriggs: "My Kinda Woman" originally appeared in *Appalachian Heritage Magazine* (2009) and subsequently in *Kaffir Lily* (Wind Publications, 2010). "Legend of Nego Mountain" originally appeared in *Appalachian Heritage Magazine* (2010) and subsequently in *How Swallowtails Become Dragons* (Accents Publishing, 2011). "I Would Make a Good Owl" originally appeared in *Still* (2012).

Jane Springer: "Salt Hill," "What We Call This Frog Hunting," "Pretty Polly," and "Whiskey Pastoral" from *Murder Ballad*. Copyright © 2012 by Jane Springer. Reprinted with the permission of The Permissions Company, Inc., on behalf of Alice James Books, www.alicejamesbooks.org.

Alex Taylor: "A Lakeside Penitence" from *The Name of the Nearest River* (Sarabande, 2010).

Jessie van Eerden: "Woman with Spirits" originally appeared under the title "Soul Catchers" in *The Oxford American*, Best of the South III, 2008.

Charles Dodd White: "Controlled Burn" originally appeared in *North Carolina Literary Review* (Summer 2010).

Jake Adam York: "Letter to Be Wrapped Around a Bottle of Whiskey" originally appeared in *Southern Quarterly* (XLVII/3). "Knoxville Girl" and "Walt Whitman in Alabama" from *Murder Ballads* (Elixir Press, 2005).

ACKNOWLEDGMENTS

We thank all of the Appalachian writers who sent us work to consider for *Red Holler*. We were surprised to find so many of you, and we're grateful for and blessed by your encouragement and inspiration. Thanks to our teachers Kevin Oderman, Gail Galloway Adams, Ethel Morgan Smith, David Muschell, Martin Lammon, Michael Griffith, Brocke Clarke, Jeffrey Skinner, and Sena Naslund, who one and all continue to inspire us and our visions. We thank our friends who have provided guidance and support: John Alleman, Kate Polak, Sasha Chernobelsky, Isabella Yu, H. M. Patterson, and Clay Matthews. We extend our gratitude to Sarah Gorham and the hard-working and wonderfully talented people at Sarabande. A special thanks also goes to Linda Bruckheimer for her support of this anthology, to John's mother Shirley Ann Lawson and his daughters Vivianne Tabbutt and Frankie Lu, to the fierce, fun-loving, and ornery people of Appalachia, and to its skies, its trees, its dogs, its ghosts, and every patch of shade and sunshine in its hollers that allowed us refuge.

THE EDITORS

John E. Branscum hails from a long line of dirt farmers, drifters, cleaning ladies, and mountain people. His poetry, fiction, and creative nonfiction have appeared in such publications as *The Evergreen Review*, *The North American Review*, and *Margin: The Journal of Magical Realism*, and he has won such awards as the Ursula LeGuin Award for Imaginative Fiction. Currently, he is the literary editor of the fashion and literature magazine *Black & Grey* and an assistant professor of Creative Writing at Indiana University of Pennsylvania.

Wayne Thomas writes fiction, nonfiction, and plays. Currently, he is the Chair of Fine Arts and teaches creative writing at Tusculum College, a small school in northeast Tennessee. He edits *The Tusculum Review*.

Sarabande Books thanks you for the purchase of this book; we do hope you enjoy it! Founded in 1994 as an independent, nonprofit, literary press, Sarabande publishes poetry, short fiction, and literary nonfiction—genres increasingly neglected by commercial publishers. We are committed to producing beautiful, lasting editions that honor exceptional writing, and to keeping those books in print. If you're interested in further reading, take a moment to browse our website, www.sarabandebooks.org. There you'll find information about other titles; opportunities to contribute to the Sarabande mission; and an abundance of supporting materials including audio, video, a lively blog, and our Sarabande in Education program.